ORPHAN GIRL & THE BAKER

VICTORIAN ROMANCE

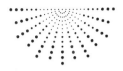

ROSIE SWAN

PUREREAD.COM

CONTENTS

CHAPTER ONE

Robert Burrows had it hard as a child, though he knew that even when times had been hardest, there had been many in Liverpool who were much worse off than himself.

He had grown up as a middle child, sandwiched between a bossy older sister and a gentle younger brother, in Vauxhall, a neighbourhood whose very name was enough to produce a shudder in most inhabitants of Liverpool, as well as those of the rest of England. Back then, during the 1840s, the junction between Vauxhall Road and Scotland Road had been riddled with cellars and courts that were barely fit for one family to live in, let alone several. Many Irish families had ended up there, too, fleeing the famine that had been wrought upon them by the very same kingdom which now rejected them and shoved them into dark corners.

Conditions in Vauxhall had been so bad that political theorists had written whole books on the subject, and it was difficult for many to believe that in a city at the heart of the greatest empire in the world, in a port city of such vital importance as Liverpool in which so much wealth was produced, there could exist such misery.

Robert had survived those days, but only barely, and most of his family had not made it out. His sister had married well. His brother, mother, and father had all died, and the effects of each loss were not always felt at the time, when the business of living had to be attended to, but rather later on, when Robert was a bit older, a bit more comfortable, and, in essence, when he had the leisure of thinking of such things.

Unlike his sister, he stayed in Liverpool, and for most of the '50s worked hard as a baker's apprentice on a street near Albert Dock. When his master, Mr. Huxby, died, he had no children to inherit his bakery and so the place passed to Robert. For the first time in his life, Robert had a responsibility other than just surviving. He had a business of his own and also the possibility of improving other people's lives. The poverty in Liverpool was nowhere near as bad now as it had been during the '40s, but it still existed, and as often as he could, Robert would go down to Albert Dock to feed the orphans.

In 1857, a year after Robert had inherited the bakery, when he was twenty-one, he went down to Albert Dock and met a little waif named Hester Grace who, from that day forward, became Robert's shadow. She started coming around to the bakery every day. She would hang around on the shop floor during the day or knock at the back door of the bakery in the evenings when Robert was having his supper. He got very used to seeing her. She never begged, though she often looked so forlorn that of course he would have to give her something. She never stole; he tested her once or twice by leaving her alone on the shop floor while he went to get something, but when he got back, the pastries and breads would still be untouched.

Hester Grace, even if she had been clad in the finest silks and jewels rather than rags and scraps, would not have ranked among the great beauties of that day. At that time, what was considered most attractive in a woman was vitality and colour, and Hester had not much of either, though there was a fascinating changeability about her brown eyes. At times they were alert with intelligence, at other times full of melting softness. The perfect curls, too, which were recommended by the fashions of the day, were not available to Hester, and her black waves of hair, which she always wore loose around her shoulders and often without any covering, would make some passersby look at her askance, while others outright ignored such a creature as beneath their notice.

For a time, Robert was unsure of Hester Grace's age. He knew that, in the couple of years that had passed since their meeting, she had grown taller, and her black hair had gotten longer, but it was not until the year that war broke out on the other side of the Atlantic, the year of 1861, that Robert learned Hester's age, because she told him one day. She had just turned eighteen. She had never known her precise birthday, but she knew that it was sometime in April, and the day that she told Robert happened to be the same day that the papers were full of announcements of the Confederacy and the Union now being at war. Neither Robert nor Hester knew then how closely that distant war would soon intertwine with their own lives. Robert gave Hester a little cake, which she ate while sitting on the steps of the back door of the bakery, and he stood beside her looking out at the yard. They talked, as they always did, of nothing in particular.

CHAPTER TWO

There was a book that Hester Grace had read once. It had been on the shelf in the schoolroom at Brownlow Hill Workhouse in Liverpool, where she had grown up. During lessons one day, she had sneaked the book under her shirt and read it that night in the girls' dormitory. She had lain curled up with her stub of a candle balanced on the bedstead and the dark roof above looming close to her face, as in the flickering light she scanned the print. There was no time for reading during the day at the workhouse. Between school in the morning and working the looms in the afternoon, there was too much to do. The end of the book made Hester want to cry, but she was afraid of waking someone up, so she just let the tears roll down her cheeks in utter silence.

The next day, when the schoolmaster was looking the other way, Hester slipped the book back onto the shelf and did not look at it again. She remembered it, all the same, and a few years later when she had been about to leave the workhouse, she had gone back to look for it, only to find that it was not in the schoolroom anymore.

The book was about a little mermaid who fell in love with a human prince, and who longed to be with him so much that she traded her voice for a pair of legs. The bargain that the little mermaid had made with the sea-witch meant that she had lost her soul, and that for every step she took on dry land, she would feel like she was walking on knives. The only way to get her soul back again would be if the prince fell in love with her, and he could not see the little mermaid as anything other than a friend. At the end of the story, he married another woman, but the little mermaid got her soul back again and became a spirit of the air. That was supposed to be her consolation, but Hester couldn't see how.

Hester did not exactly feel like she was walking on knives whenever she was with him, her prince, who was really a baker called Robert, but sometimes she felt like she couldn't breathe, and sometimes she felt afraid of how quickly time seemed to pass when they were together. It made her wonder if one day this time that they had together might run out. That was why Hester liked to observe Robert every now and then, through the bakery window as he talked to customers, or from on top of the neighbour's wall as he walked up Cobbler's Lane. She would watch as he picked up the ball some children were playing with and threw it back to them, or as he stopped to help old Alice Smith carry her shopping. When Hester was not with Robert but instead watching him from a distance, time seemed to pass more normally. She could hear his laugh and see his smile, and she did not feel so afraid that she would lose those things someday.

Robert Burrows really looked quite ordinary until you had seen him smile for the first time. after that, even when he looked sad or serious, it was hard not to think of that smile. The possibility of it seemed to change his face completely. Once you had seen Robert smile, he transformed from a young man with a mop of brown, curly hair, to a handsome prince with light in his eyes, or so it seemed to Hester Grace, at least. She did not know whether anyone else saw him the way that she did. It wasn't until one day in October 1861, when a visitor came to Liverpool to see Robert, that Hester really began to feel, for the first time, in danger of losing her prince.

Hester was walking up Cobbler's Lane, towards the bakery, when she bumped into someone. She had been out scavenging in Albert Dock that morning, and she was still carrying an old sack full of cans, bits of rope, and other things. The stuff rattled as she ran headlong into a gentleman, and he started apologising right away.

"Never mind, sir," said Hester, bowing her head so that her hair came down to cover her face, and holding the sack behind her back.

"No, really, I wasn't watching where I was going." The gentleman sounded like he was from Manchester. Hester peered up at him curiously. He was fair and thin, with a receding hairline. He looked up and down the lane before going on, "The truth is, I'm a bit lost. Can you tell me if Burrows' bakery is anywhere nearby?"

"Yes, sir, it's right down that way," said Hester at once, pointing. "Happens I'm going there myself. I can show you." She hadn't really been planning to stop at the bakery, but this gentleman looked so gormless that she thought she'd better show him where it was, and if she got to see Robert into the bargain, then so much the better.

"Oh, that's very kind, thank you." They fell into step together and she sensed the gentleman glance at her. "So, do you know Mr. Burrows?"

"Know him? Oh, yes, sir, I often go around to his shop. He's been very kind to me."

"Yes, Robert is very kind." The Manchester gentleman cleared his throat as though embarrassed. "My name is Cecil Locksmith. I'm Robert's brother-in-law."

"Ah, so you're the one as owns the great warehouse in Manchester?" Hester exclaimed.

"Er, yes, that's right." Mr. Locksmith sounded more embarrassed than ever, so Hester decided it would be wiser to drop the subject of the warehouse. At any rate, they were approaching the door of the bakery. She stepped back to let the gentleman enter first, and, bafflingly, he did the same.

"Ladies first," he said after a moment, and Hester smiled and raised her eyebrows as she pushed open the door of the bakery. It was the first time in her life that anyone had ever called her a lady.

"Hester!" Robert sang out from behind the counter. A smile had broken out on his face as soon as he saw her, and when the gentleman entered behind her, that smile turned to a positive beam. "And Cecil! Well, this is a surprise!"

The other customers turned around to look at them, too, and Hester shrank back into the corner so that people wouldn't look at her too long. She wasn't exactly wearing her Sunday best. Robert served the last few customers before coming around from behind the counter to give Cecil a hearty shake of the hand. "Well, sir, so how do you do? I hope you had a comfortable journey from Manchester?"

"Very comfortable, thank you. I thought I'd drop in before my meeting and see how you were."

"I hope you didn't come out of your way!"

"Not out of my way at all. The meeting is just down on Albert Dock."

"How is Lesley? And how're the children?"

"They're well, all well, thank you."

Hester had started inching towards the door, not wanting to disturb the reunion now that her job was done. What happened next was the strangest thing. – One minute the two men were talking, and the next minute one of them, the brother-in-law, had buckled over, nearly overbalancing. Robert grabbed hold of him and struggled to keep him upright, his apron bunching up under Mr. Locksmith's weight as he exclaimed, "Help! Help! Won't someone help?"

The apprentice, Marcus, came darting out from behind the counter with a chair, which he and Robert managed to get Mr. Locksmith onto. The gentleman seemed to be half-conscious still. His mouth was open, and Hester could see the whites of his eyes under his lids, but his colour was awful, all white and grey.

"The meeting," Mr. Locksmith murmured, and made as if to get out of the chair. Robert put a hand on his chest to restrain him, leaving a trail of flour on the man's black waistcoat. "No. I'm all right, really. I just didn't eat very much today. and it was so hot on the train."

"You're not going anywhere until you've seen a surgeon," Robert said firmly. Turning back to his apprentice, who was hopping from one foot to the other in his agitation, he said, "Marcus, you know where Mr. Russell lives, on Lime Street? Go fetch him, please."

"Yes, Mr. Burrows," said Marcus, and took off his apron before rushing out of the bakery. As he was going, he turned the sign on the door from 'Open' to 'Closed'. From her corner, Hester stepped forward, the wares in her bag rattling.

"You said this meeting is down on Albert Dock, sir?"

Both men looked startled at the sound of her voice, as though they had forgotten she was there. "Yes," Mr. Locksmith said after a moment, and grimaced. "It's in the building next to the Dock Office, at the headquarters of a trading company, Fairbank & Co."

"Fairbank," Hester repeated, and then nodded. "I know it. I shall go send word you've been taken ill."

She turned and made for the door. Robert's voice floated after her as she was going, a faint, distracted, "Thank you, Hester."

Marcus came back a half-hour later with Mr. Russell in tow. He was a good lad, Marcus. He had started apprenticing with Robert last year, at fifteen, the same age Robert had been when he started here back in '51, when the bakery had belonged to Mr. Huxby, who had since died and whose wife no longer lived in Liverpool. The Huxbys had no children, so the bakery had passed to Robert and since then, it had been his to manage alone.

People often told Robert that he ought to get a wife who would help him run the place, but when Robert Burrows thought of marriage, he thought of his own parents. He thought of slammed doors and broken bottles. He looked at his brother-in-law, Cecil, stretched out now on the settee in the back room, and saw only a tired, faded man, a man who had tried and failed to make a success of himself. The last time Robert had seen his sister Lesley, when he had visited them in Manchester, she had looked worn out, too, and she had spent every spare minute trying to stop little Mary and Sam from bickering. On those rare occasions during that visit when she had actually spoken to Robert, it had been solely to complain about Cecil. So, in short, Robert did not look on marriage as something that would solve any of his problems, but rather as a grim eventuality that he need not think about just yet.

"I'm sorry," said Cecil after the surgeon had left. Robert looked down at the settee to see his brother-in-law watching him. "You had to close up shop on my account."

"It's one day, Cecil." Robert waved a floury hand. "It makes little difference. Besides, Marcus is going to see to it that whatever we didn't sell today is brought down to Albert Dock. Aren't you, Marcus?" He raised his voice slightly so that his apprentice, lingering by the open door, had no choice but to hear him.

"But, Mr. Burrows, I don't like those children as run around barefoot and steals things."

"They don't steal. Most of them don't, in any case. They scavenge, and they often go hungry at this time of day." Robert watched with a half-smile as Marcus stumped out of the room.

"It seems things haven't changed all that much in this town," Cecil sighed, adjusting his position on the settee. "When I worked here, I used to hate going down the docks, same as your apprentice. I hated seeing the children going hungry. That was back during the '40s, of course. You'll remember, Rob, how bad things were then."

"I remember," said Robert. He walked around the table where he had used to eat all his meals with Mr. Huxby, a table that was only ever laid for one person these days, since Marcus took his meals at home. Untying his apron and slinging it on the chair, he said over his shoulder, "Maybe there aren't as many kids around Albert Dock these days. But still, you can't help feeling it when you see them."

"Is that girl, Hester, one of them?"

"Hester?" Robert repeated and turned back to face Cecil with a smile. He leaned one hand on the back of a chair as he thought for a moment. "She *was*. Now I suppose she still goes down there, but she's not like those other poor kids. She's clever, and she makes things."

"Makes things? What do you mean?"

"I mean, she, well, I don't know." Robert came around the table again, feeling he was quite out of his depth now. "She finds all kinds of odds and ends down at the docks. Sometimes she brings them around here to show me. Tins, forks, candelabras, even violin strings once. Ordinary things, mostly, but she makes something new out of them and tries to sell them. She can fix things, too, like that." He pointed to the round clock that hung above the door separating the back room from the kitchen. "It used to always lag a few minutes behind, no matter how much I wound it up. I let Hester at it and now it's always on the hour, every hour. Listen."

The large hand had just joined the small hand at four o'clock, and in the quiet came the distant chiming of the bells at St Nicholas's. Cecil Locksmith's eyes widened, and for a moment he looked as though he might even smile, but then his face settled back into its customary weary expression and he said in a low voice, "Extraordinary. Though, speaking of timekeeping, oughtn't your Hester be back from Fairbank's by now? Do you think she got lost?"

"I doubt it," said Robert after a moment. "She knows Liverpool like the back of her hand." With a glance at the clock, "But you're right, it has been a while. Almost two hours."

"There's nothing for it. I shall go myself and explain to them what happened." Cecil made to get up, but Robert restrained him by the shoulder.

"Mr. Russell said you were to rest."

"I have rested. And I've eaten, too, and that was all that was the matter with me, really."

Robert kept his hold on his brother-in-law's shoulder. Even if Cecil had been in his full health, Robert would have had the advantage on him in strength. As it was, he was easy to restrain. After a moment, Cecil gave up and squeezed his eyes shut.

"What's so important about this meeting, anyway?" Robert asked, letting go of Cecil's shoulder. As his brother-in-law threw him a withering look, he sighed. "That is, I mean, why should you risk your health for a meeting? You're evidently not well enough to travel."

"I told you, there's nothing the matter with me. Anyway, you only get one chance with Harold Fairbank." Cecil stared up at the ceiling, the expression in his grey eyes intense. "I have to get this deal."

They both listened to the ticking of the clock for a moment. "Are things that bad in Manchester, then?" Robert asked finally, in a low voice.

"Things are bad all over the country," said Cecil, and he seemed on the point of saying more when there came the tinkle of the shop bell. Robert sighed and got to his feet.

"I shall go and tell them we're closed," he said over his shoulder to Cecil as he went. "Though I don't know how they could have missed the sign on the door." He stopped talking as soon as he saw who was standing in the shop, and he came to a dead halt behind the counter. His hands jumped up to his hair, then down to his apron, wiping them there even though they were already clean as they could be.

A young lady was standing just inside the door, if young lady she could be called, for surely there was a title more noble, more worthy of the vision of beauty that greeted Robert's eyes at that moment. Her hair was brown touched with gold, teased into soft ringlets that framed her heart-shaped face. She was not dressed in the extravagant, loud patterns worn by many of the other young ladies of status in Liverpool. Her dress, instead, was plain blue trimmed with black, but something about the depth of colour and texture of the fabric told Robert that it had been just as costly as any of those other fine ladies' dresses. Her eyes danced with good humour, and the older gentleman standing beside her, evidently her father, wore the same expression, but Robert only afforded him a glance or two before looking back at the young lady. He thought, and the thought was met with a kind of rising panic within him, that he might never be able to take his eyes off her.

"Is Mr. Locksmith here?" the gentleman asked finally, his brown moustache quivering as he spoke. His eyes now had narrowed slightly as he considered Robert. "We were told-"

"Yes," Robert burst out, surprising himself with his capacity for speech. "Yes, he's here. I shall go and-" He looked back one last time at the young lady, who was smiling now, before he turned towards the back door. "I shall go and fetch him."

CHAPTER THREE

I t had taken Hester quite a while to find Mr.
Fairbank. He had not been at his offices on the
docks, and neither had his secretary there been
particularly helpful. As soon as he spotted Hester coming
up to his desk, he seemed anxious to get her out of the
place as soon as possible. On her way there, she had
stowed away the sack of scavenged items in her secret
spot, in the loft of an abandoned warehouse, and she had
combed through her dark hair with her fingers, but she
couldn't do much about the fact that she had no shoes, or
the fact that the streets of Liverpool were black with mud
at this time of year.

"He might be at the post office on Duke Street," the
secretary said, his eyes fixed on some point behind Hester,
where a trail of muddy footsteps led across the tiled floor
to the door through which she had entered. "There's a
delivery due to come in this evening and he always checks

at the post office in case of delays. Or perhaps he's at his solicitor's office in Toxteth. Or at his sister's house."

"And where is that?" Hester said, after an expectant pause. The secretary looked at her warily.

"West Derby Road."

"Thank you." She was about to leave when a thought struck her, and she turned back. The secretary looked pained. "Beg your pardon, sir, but wasn't Mr. Fairbank supposed to be in a meeting at this time?"

"He has no meetings scheduled for today," the secretary said, with a cursory glance at the black book on the edge of his desk.

"Alright," said Hester. "Well, I shall check all those places for him, then." And she proceeded to do exactly that.

The post office on Duke Street was closest, and though the place was so crowded that the windows were beginning to steam up, the postmistress told Hester that Mr. Fairbank had made no appearance there today. Toxteth was a bit of a longer walk, and by the time she got there it had started to drizzle rain. Hester tried the street door of the solicitor's office and found that it was locked. She peered up at the blurry grey sky and then bent her steps towards the north of the city.

There were many houses on West Derby Road, and she tried six in succession before finding the one where Mr. Fairbank's sister lived. Thankfully, the gentleman in question was there, and the maid told Hester to wait in the kitchen while she went to deliver her message about Mr. Locksmith. While Hester was waiting, the cook gave her some bread-and-butter, which was a good thing as she was starting to feel very hungry by then. The maid came back down and told her that Mr. Fairbank was very sorry. He had completely forgotten about meeting Mr. Locksmith today.

"He's going straight to Cobbler's Lane now to see him, and to make his apologies in person." The maid looked down at Hester's muddied feet and then added, "He's bringing the carriage. If you want to save yourself the walk, you can hop up in front. Better hurry, though."

Hester did hurry. She burst outside just as Mr. Fairbank was emerging from the front door, and she hung back a respectful distance until he had made his way to the carriage. She saw that he was not alone, but with a young lady in a dark blue gown trimmed with black, whom Hester assumed to be his daughter. Hester watched until they had disappeared into the carriage, and then hurried to sit up front.

The coachman was young, probably only around Hester's age, with a round friendly face and fair curly hair. He kept asking her questions about herself as they drove through the streets, but she did not pay him much mind. Her thoughts were full of Robert. He must be worried by now. He would think she hadn't been able to find Mr. Fairbank. She thought of the relieved smile that would cross his face when he saw them arriving at the bakery. She thought of the look of grateful surprise that she had seen in his eyes a few times before, each time a precious memory, as each time she had seen it, it had been for her and her alone. She wondered if she would see that look again today. She hoped that she would. She hoped so hard that it hurt something inside her.

Cobbler's Lane was too narrow for a carriage, so they stopped at the bottom of Dale Street, and the Fairbanks got out to walk. Hester thanked the coachman distractedly and followed after them, once again keeping a respectful distance. She did not know whether they knew she was there. She thought that they mustn't know, but then at one point Miss Fairbank looked back and saw her. She smiled and said something to her father, and Hester, embarrassed, ducked into a doorway before he could turn around and look at her.

She would just see that they got to the right place, she decided. She wouldn't go in and talk to Robert. He would have enough on his mind, in any case. Keeping a greater distance between them than before, she followed the Fairbanks down Cobbler's Lane, descending until the white dome of the Dock Office had disappeared behind the rooftops. She passed the rag-and-bone shop, whose bent-backed proprietor, Alice Smith, was sweeping up the front step, regardless of the rain. She passed the tiny bookstand and glanced down at the book covers just as she always did, inadvertently meeting the gaze of the old bookseller in the process. She smiled, but he did not smile back. He never did.

Hester drew up to the bakery just as the swing of Miss Fairbank's crinoline had disappeared inside the door. Mr. Fairbank followed after her, and Hester took up a position at one of the side windows, peering over a display of scones to the scene within. She saw Robert come out from behind the counter and wipe his hands on his apron. She saw the astounded look on his face as soon as he had clapped eyes on Miss Fairbank. He looked like a man waking up from a long sleep, his eyes very wide and blinking rapidly, the usual ruddiness of his complexion changing to a darker crimson.

Backing away from the bakery window, Hester suddenly understood why the little mermaid in the story had always felt like she was walking on knives when she was with her prince. Every step that she put between herself and Robert felt like it was straining tighter and tighter a cord that tied her heart to his, and yet there was no way she could stay and watch, not now that she had seen that look in his eyes. Hester kept backing away, almost limping in her agony, and did not notice what was behind her until she had knocked right into it.

"You, girl!" cried the bookseller, rushing out from behind the stand. Hester looked down at the books she had knocked to the ground and then back at the bookseller's livid face, before she took off running. His shouts echoed after her all the way up to the top of Cobbler's Lane.

CHAPTER FOUR

Mr. Harold Fairbank was very apologetic that he had forgotten about the meeting, and to make up for his absentmindedness, he offered to talk with Cecil there and then in the bakery. Robert showed him into the back room and shut the door firmly behind them, and then he drew in a breath, what felt like the first he had taken in the past half hour, before going out to talk to Miss Fairbank.

Simona was her first name, he had discovered from hearing her father address her, and he couldn't think of a lovelier or more fitting one. She was sitting now, on the chair that Robert had found her, and he came around the counter as they spoke but stayed standing. She told him about his father's business, about how the war in America had not affected them as badly as it had affected others around the country, thank goodness, though who knew how things might change if it dragged on for years and years. Robert murmured his agreement and looked down at the floor, only chancing the occasional glance up at her as she went on speaking. He had to remind himself repeatedly to focus on her words, for as he listened to her soft, refined tones, it was hard not to let his mind wander. Miss Fairbank had barely any accent. She might have passed for any young lady from London if not for the way that Liverpool dipped in to colour every odd word that dropped from her tongue, but she seemed all the lovelier for that. Robert, in those occasional glances up, noticed other imperfections as they went on talking. He saw that one of her front teeth was a little crooked, and that her ringlets were beginning to get a little limp in the damp, warm air of the bakery. with each imperfection that he noticed, his heart would start to beat faster and faster, for it was easier, after all, and infinitely more frightening, to fall in love with a mortal being than with a vision of beauty.

He told Miss Fairbank what little there was to tell about his own life, his childhood growing up in Vauxhall Road, which was still one of the poorest neighbourhoods in Liverpool, how his older sister Lesley had fallen in love with Cecil Locksmith back when he had been a clerk working in a flour mill in Toxteth, and how Lesley and Cecil had then moved to Manchester, where Cecil had opened his warehouse.

"Did you ever think of moving to Manchester, too?" Miss Fairbank interjected in her gentle voice. "I'm sure your brother-in-law could find you work as a foreman or perhaps a clerk."

Robert had never so much as considered moving to Manchester, but now he found himself blinking at her and saying, "Well, yes, I suppose he could, though I like working here. I like running a place that's my own. I don't have to answer to anyone."

He thought he saw something like disappointment in her eyes then, and hastened to add, "Though of course, if I ever get tired of the bakery, it's good to have another possibility."

"Of course," she said, a little stiffly, and they both glanced towards the back-room door, beyond which they could hear the low voices of Mr. Fairbank and Cecil still conversing.

"Seems that they have quite a lot to talk about," Robert said after a moment's pause.

"It's always the same with my father's meetings, and he's been having of them lately." Miss Fairbank turned her eyes back on Robert, and she seemed to be aware of making some kind of impression as she went on, "Everyone wants my father's cotton. Most of the other brokers sourced their cotton from the American South before the war broke out there, you see, and that's why they're in trouble now, but my father has always had his own suppliers in Egypt and India."

"That's fortunate," said Robert, who was feeling a little out of his depth now. "And do you often accompany your father to his meetings?"

He expected her to blush and demur, but instead she nodded, still quite solemn, and said, "Oh, yes. He likes to have me around so he can talk about the deals with me afterwards. He says that I have always had a head for this kind of business. He says that it is a pity I was not born a boy."

"Do you wish you'd been born a boy?" said Robert lightly, with the feeling of being back on familiar ground, and this time Miss Fairbank did blush and laugh a little.

"Oh, well, no, of course not." And what did that glance up at him mean, so fleeting that he would have missed it had he so much as blinked? Robert was used to how warm it could get in here, but now he was beginning to feel that the heat on his face was almost unbearable.

They got around to talking about books. Robert hadn't read much besides a few Dickens. His sister Lesley had always been the reader in their family, and, without lying outright, he tried to follow along as best as he could as Miss Fairbank described the various writers she liked. He tried, too, to give the impression that, even if he had not read any of the books she was talking about, he was at least aware of them. At the first break in their conversation, he mentioned the bookstand up the street and suggested that they walk along and look at it.

The cool air felt wonderful on his face. Beneath their feet, the cobblestones were slippery from the recent rain, and Miss Fairbank stepped very carefully, placing one slippered foot in front of the other. Robert glanced at her once or twice as they walked, but just to check that she was keeping her balance, certainly not to admire her button nose in profile.

At the bookstand, Mr. Moss glared at them and did not answer their "Good afternoons.". "He's always like that," Robert said in an undertone to Miss Fairbank, who appeared in any case to be distracted by a volume of Thackeray's, whom she had just been discussing back in the bakery. As she picked up the book and began to flick through the pages, Robert looked over the other books on display for something that he could at least pretend to be interested in. In the process, he met the gaze of the bookseller again, and Mr. Moss, still glaring, actually shuffled forward now to address him.

"Well?" the old man said, as though picking up in the middle of a conversation that Robert hadn't been aware they were having. "Where is she?"

Ordinarily, Robert would have laughed and told him to come off it. Mr. Moss's eccentricities were well-known to him, but with Miss Fairbank within earshot, he was conscious of the need to appear more mannerly, and so he asked very calmly, "I beg your pardon, sir? Where is who?"

"The girl," grumbled the bookseller, "the girl who's always slinking around your bakery."

Out of the corner of his eye, Robert saw Miss Fairbank look up from her book. He felt his face beginning to warm again, despite the cool air.

"Oh, you must mean Hester," he said after a moment.

"Whatever her name is, she came tearing by here not half an hour ago and knocked over my Lawrence Sterne. I have it drying out inside now." The bookseller nodded to the building behind him, whose tiny cellar Robert knew to comprise the man's whole lodgings. The rest of it was given over to a draper's shop. "Next time I see her, I'll have a few words to say to her, oh, yes."

"Who is this you're talking about?" Miss Fairbank, with a swish of skirts, had come forward to Robert's side. Glancing from the bookseller to her, Robert did his best to explain who Hester Grace was, though he didn't have much more success than when he had tried to do the same with Cecil.

"She was the one who went to fetch your father," he wound up by explaining. Then, with a frown, "At least, I think she must have been, though it seems she didn't stick around after you arrived."

"Perhaps she was shy." Miss Fairbank was smiling now. Was it really a smile of relief? Robert had to look at her twice to make sure he wasn't imagining things. Why should Miss Fairbank be relieved that the girl Mr. Moss had been talking about was only an orphan from the docks? Unless... Robert's mind leapt through several wonderful possibilities in the space of a few seconds.

"Well, you tell her when you see her that she's to come back here."

"Yes, Mr. Moss," said Robert, and suffused with the glow of Miss Fairbank's regard, for she had now turned that smile on him, he managed to sound dignified and humorous and apologetic all at the same time.

They walked back to the bakery rather than dawdling any more at the bookstand, for Miss Fairbank, with that uncanny sense of timing that must have come from years of accompanying her father to meetings, said that things would likely be wrapping up soon, and sure enough, they had not been back five minutes when both gentlemen emerged from the back room. Mr. Fairbank was still wearing the same good-humoured expression that he'd had when he first arrived, so it was impossible to tell just by looking at him how the meeting had gone, but Robert, in response to the quick, inquiring glance he sent Cecil, got a tired smile and a tiny nod. He really had to stop himself from beaming outright then, because everything this afternoon seemed to be going right. Beyond Cecil's fainting, of course, though somehow that seemed like a distant memory, Robert hadn't known that it was possible for such a perfect afternoon to exist.

Mr. Fairbank took his leave first of Cecil and then of Robert with a hearty handshake each, and Miss Fairbank curtsied. Watching them walk out of his bakery, up the street and out of sight, Robert felt the warm glow inside him begin to be dissolved by a kind of black mist which was not quite despair. Maybe dismay would have been a better word, though alone it didn't seem strong enough, as it struck him that he had no guarantee that he would see Simona Fairbank again, no way of finding her beyond hunting down the address of her father's office in Albert Dock, and that, even if he were to do that, he had no idea whether such a pursuit would be acceptable to her or not. She had not even looked him in the eye when they were saying goodbye. Probably she had been just passing the time with him; probably she met many workmen in the course of her father's business and hadn't seen Robert any differently from them.

"Well, that's a weight off my mind," said Cecil with a sigh, "though I never really believe a thing until I see it in writing. He said he'd send the documents to Manchester for me to sign, so I'll hold my breath till then. I suppose I'd better get going if I want to catch the six o'clock train."

"You shouldn't travel anywhere today," said Robert, speaking distractedly, for his eyes had just alighted on a pair of lady's blue gloves that had been left on the empty display shelf beside the chair where Miss Fairbank had been sitting. "Not after your fit earlier. Stay tonight and go back on the first train tomorrow."

"Really, Robert, you're making a fuss over nothing," Cecil started to say, but Robert had already made his way around the counter and did not stay to hear the rest of his brother-in-law's sentence. He seized up the pair of gloves and rushed out the door. Halfway up Cobbler's Lane, he met Miss Fairbank, who was out of breath and alone.

"Thank you! How careless of me." As she took the gloves from him, she smiled at Robert in such a way as gave him to understand that it had not been careless of her at all. "I must go back. Father is waiting in the carriage."

"Of course," said Robert, a little breathless himself, and Miss Fairbank made to turn away. Then, looking back at him, she said,

"We live very near my father's office. Number 5, Canning Place. If you wanted to send me a message some time, it would be to that address. But it would have to be very discreet, through someone you trust. My father, you know, wouldn't approve if he knew."

"Of course," said Robert again, too happy in that moment to do anything other than accept her father's disapproval of him as an unalterable truth.

"Well, then," said Miss Fairbank, still hesitating a moment more. She smiled at him before she turned to go. "Good day."

CHAPTER FIVE

All Hester wanted to do now was keep away. She had never felt that before, not in the years that she had known Robert. Ever since she had first seen him smile, as he was handing out yesterday's loaves to the scavengers on Albert Dock, her days had fixed themselves around him. Those days had once been long and formless. Now he became the centre of pulsating light around which they revolved. Other people matched their movements to the rising and setting of the sun; Hester, from then on, matched her movements to Robert's. She knew, of course, that his smile on that first day hadn't been for her, that to him, hers had been just another dirty face amid a group of orphans, but when she had started seeking him out, when she had come sidling up to the door of his bakery to introduce herself, then he had started smiling just for her.

She must have been braver back then, at fourteen. If she were to meet Robert for the first time now, Hester wasn't sure if she would ever have worked up the courage to talk to him. But back then, she hadn't known anything about the fear that came with love. She hadn't known that the more you got, the more you were afraid of losing. She had only ever gotten smiles from Robert, smiles and kind words, but even those she had jealously guarded, and until today she had never seen him rendered speechless in the presence of a young lady.

Maybe it wasn't exactly about courage, though, Hester reflected as she stood on a corner on Lime Street. She watched the stream of gentlemen released from their offices for the day, cotton brokers, moneylenders, and managers, most of them too occupied in their conversations to notice her holding out her tin. They were talking to each other about where they would go for dinner, about letters received and meetings to be arranged, and as her eyes followed them down the street, she wondered if there was more of greed than fear in what she felt for Robert. Was it really true that over the years, she had gotten afraid of losing what she already had, his good opinion, his friendship, or had she just gotten greedy?

She should be able to go back there and face him, Hester decided as she shook out the contents of the tin into her palm and saw that she had gotten sixpence. She put the tin into the pocket of her greatcoat, where it made an odd bulge, and set off walking down a street that was now nearly empty. Night was falling, all the more quickly since it had been such a grey day, but Hester wasn't going to skulk around like a wounded animal anymore. She would go back to Cobbler's Lane to see how Mr. Locksmith was getting on, and whether his meeting with Mr. Fairbank had gone off well. If, in doing so, she had to hear about other meetings, then so be it. Robert Burrows had been good to her, and he would be expecting to see her now. She couldn't just disappear.

In the end, they settled that Cecil should stay the night at the bakery before travelling back to Manchester the following day. He retired early, taking the bed in Robert's small room upstairs, and Robert put a pillow and a blanket on the settee in the back room but couldn't persuade himself to lie down just yet. He normally got in a few hours' sleep before getting up at one to set the dough. He knew that it would be prudent, especially since he had lost some business today, to get as much rest as he could so as to prepare for a busy day tomorrow, but he kept pacing around the bakery, checking things that he knew had been checked already. The shop door was locked, the book-keeping pad had been put away, and the oil lamp in the back room was in no danger of running out of fuel any time soon. Robert didn't even know what he had been waiting for, didn't know how much he had been itching to tell someone about the events of the day, until he heard a furtive knock at the back door and dashed to answer it.

"Hester!" The light from the oil lamp illuminated her pale skin, made all the paler by her dark overcoat and waves of black hair that framed her face. Robert tugged her inside by the forearm and had her sit at the table. "Will you have something to eat?"

Hester looked a little dazed, and rather than put her to the trouble of responding, Robert said, "I'll get you some bread-and-butter." He rummaged around the cupboards as quietly as he could, so as not to disturb Cecil upstairs, and set the plate in front of her a few minutes later, along with a glass of ale. He sat opposite her at the table, watching as she ate and drank. Under his gaze, she seemed to be move very carefully, and every now and then, before taking a bite of bread or a sup of ale, her solemn brown eyes would rise to meet his, as though she expected him to reprimand her.

"You're later than usual," Robert said at last, thinking that a little conversation might put her at her ease, and not yet seeing how he could delicately steer into his desired subject. Hester nodded as she chewed.

"I didn't get as much at the pawnshop as I was hoping."

"For the things you scavenged?"

She nodded again, a chunk of dark hair falling over her high forehead. "But I'm working on something new."

"Another of your inventions?" said Robert, eagerly, and Hester gave him another one of those furtive glances. "Tell me more."

"I won't till it's finished," she said, her voice quiet but firm.

"Just like always." Robert settled back in his chair, unsurprised by her answer. "Anyway, you'll be glad to hear the deal went off."

"So Mr. Fairbank is going to sell your brother-in-law cotton?"

"That's right. And it's thanks to you that they had the meeting at all. You saved us, Hester." Robert looked at her properly then, not a momentary glance but a lingering look, as he tried his best to communicate that a little more lay behind his words, more than he felt he could express at that moment. Hester gazed back at him, but he couldn't tell by her expression alone whether or not she understood. He forced himself to go on. "And there's something else that I wanted to ask you. If you could go somewhere, bring a message, but only if it's on your way home, and only if you can."

Hester held his gaze and said, "Tell me."

Robert hesitated for a moment. "Do you promise not to tell anyone about this? Anyone other than, I mean, other than her."

Hester nodded, and he sighed in relief. "Thank you. It's about,– well, it's about Mr. Fairbank's daughter Simona."

CHAPTER SIX

The Albert Dock had been Hester's home pretty much since she had left Brownlow Hill Workhouse at twelve years old. Back then, because she had finished her schooling a little earlier than the other children her age, the overseers had sent her out, alone, to be apprenticed at a dressmaker's shop on Castle Street. Hester had only lasted a month in that place before running away. The dressmaker, Mrs. Sharp, had worked her from dawn to dusk and made her sleep on a hard floor at night. Hester was clever with cogs and wheels but hopeless with a needle and thread, and whenever she cut herself and ended up bleeding over a piece of work, Mrs. Sharp would give her a beating instead of something to dress her wounds.

Though she had been worked hard and brought up rough in Brownlow Hill, Hester was unaccustomed to outright cruelty. One morning, while Mrs. Sharp was out attending to a delivery, she had made a run for it. She had very nearly gone back to the workhouse, as they had told her to do if she was ill-treated, but standing outside the gates, looking up at the vast facade with its many turrets and gables, Hester had felt her heart sinking in her chest like a stone in water. She didn't want to face the governor's questions, and she didn't want to face the possibility of having to go back to Castle Street. She turned and made for the docks instead, with the foolish idea of boarding a ship, even though at that time she hadn't two pennies to rub together. There she had met some other kids like her, who had run away from home or from the workhouse or, as in her case, from a cruel master or mistress. They lived on what they could find, debris from forgotten or abandoned crates amid the tonnes of cargo that passed through the docks every day. Some stole, but Hester didn't. She saw the heavy price paid by those who were caught stealing. The girls were sent to correction houses, the boys put on juvenile reformatory ships. In her time living here, she ended up saying goodbye to many friends that way. Others left of their own accord, stowing away on ships for better chances abroad. A few disappeared without a trace.

The new generation of scavengers, as Hester had started to think of them, seemed tougher and meaner than the one in which she had come up. There were fewer of them, and they stuck together in tighter gangs. Their various dens were dotted all up and down the docks, in alleys, cellars, and garrets. They stole as well as scavenged and, unlike so many of Hester's friends in the past, were smart enough not to get caught while doing it. Hester tried her best to keep away from them, but this was easier said than done when they all hung around the same patch.

She had just left Robert at the bakery and was nearing the bottom of Cobbler's Lane when she felt the hairs at the back of her neck start to prickle. Hester squared her shoulders and felt in the pocket of her greatcoat for one of the rocks that she always carried with her. Then, instead of going straight on, she made a sharp turn right into a blind alley and felt her way to the doorway that she knew to be there. She stepped back to make sure she was utterly concealed in its shadows and listened for the sound of footsteps along the wet cobbles.

They came a minute or two later, very light footsteps, almost soundless, evidently belonging to a very light creature, and they halted for a moment as if in indecision before turning into the alley. Hester lunged forward and seized the bony shoulders of her pursuer, and a brief struggle in the dark ensued before she managed to drag him out into the open. There, under the oily illumination of a streetlamp, she saw a skinny boy in a blue frock coat and tartan trousers that were so big, the material pooled at his ankles.

"Gentleman Fred," she greeted, keeping a firm grip on his collar even as she lowered the rock in her other hand. "What do you want? Why are you following me?"

Fred Small, also known around the docks as Gentleman Fred for his predilection for wearing fine clothes and speaking in a hoity-toity way, attempted to wriggle out of her grip for another minute or two before finally answering, in slightly choked tones, "I assure you, Miss Grace, no discourtesy was meant. Now if you would kindly let me go…"

"Did Billy Ross send you?" she demanded, without loosening her grip.

"No. In fact, I have broken with Mr. Ross and struck out on my own."

"Hmph. I'll believe that when I see it."

"You are looking at a free man, Miss Grace, a man unbound by pacts or obligations."

"You're not a man," Hester scoffed, but she let go of his collar all the same. Fred Small sprang away a few steps, righting the collar of his coat and patting down the material before turning back to face her. She went on, "You're just a kid. Anyway, if Billy Ross didn't send you to tail me, then what is it? What do you want?"

Fred Small said nothing for a minute, patting the straw-coloured hair at the top of his head as though expecting to find a hat there. He looked a little disappointed when his hand came away empty, and he met Hester's inquiring gaze with an innocent expression. "Where are you going? Home?"

"None of your business," she retorted, quick as a flash.

He looked unsurprised by her response. "If you're going home, you might want to watch out. You put up in Davies's old warehouse, don't you?"

"Where I put up is none of your business."

"Well, Miss Grace, all the same, consider this a courteous warning. There is a mysterious vessel moored beside Davies's."

"A 'mysterious vessel'!" repeated Hester, almost laughing at the absurdity of it. "No one's used that warehouse in years. I was there just this afternoon, and I didn't see any ship."

"She sailed in with nightfall," said Fred Small portentously. "And now she's sitting silent, waiting. There's crates and crates of something on board, I saw them with my own eyes, God only knows what they hold."

"Cotton, probably," said Hester. "Or coffee, or tobacco, or whatever else they usually trade here. It's no mystery."

"But why wait till nightfall to unload her wares?" Fred questioned, widening those sly eyes of his. He glanced up and down the deserted street and lowered his voice. "If you ask me, it has something to do with the black market. And if this cargo has been shipped to be dealt in the black market, then it wouldn't exactly be wrong to displace a crate or two, now, would it?"

"Don't tell me you and Billy Ross are going to get mixed up in this."

"I told you, Miss Grace, I work alone now. However, if you were interested in joining me in investigating this mysterious cargo, you would be welcome to reap some of the benefits of –"

"No," said Hester, flatly. Fred Small, who, in his excitement, had been straining up to get his face level with hers, sank back down on his heels. "Thank you for the warning, Small. I'll find somewhere else to sleep tonight. And I advise you to stay well away from Davies's till this 'mystery vessel' is gone." She continued down the street, calling back over her shoulder, "And don't even think about following me this time!"

All the way to Canning Place, Hester kept her ears strained for the sound of light footsteps, but heard only silence, and was forced to acknowledge that Gentleman Fred had enough good sense to heed some, if not all, of her words. She stopped outside Number 5, the address that Robert had given her. The house was modest enough, which was unsurprising given the part of town they were in. Hester wondered, absently, why Mr. Fairbank didn't move out to the north-east like most of the other big merchants and tradesmen had done. By the looks of it, everyone in the house had already gone to bed, but when she pushed open the small gate and went around the side, she saw that the light was still on in the servants' quarters. She rapped at the door, paused, and then rapped again.

While Hester waited, she began, for the first time, to feel the creeping, damp cold. How had she not noticed it before? It seemed to settle on every part of her, from her hairline down to her bare toes. The next time she saw Gentleman Fred, Hester decided, she would ask if he could pilfer a pair of boots for her. They could be any size; it didn't matter if they chafed or pinched, just as long as they covered her feet. Otherwise she would freeze to death come winter. Normally she wouldn't want to share in Gentleman Fred's ill-gotten gains, but who was going to miss a pair of old boots?

It comforted Hester a little to think about these things, especially after such a day, such a long day as Hester didn't know if she'd ever had before. She felt as if, from dawn to dusk, her heart had shrunk and expanded several sizes. A few hours ago she had been convinced she could never go to Robert's bakery again, that it would hurt her too badly. And it had hurt, but here she was, still standing. She wondered if, after all, it was only in stories that someone could die of a broken heart. Maybe that was the terrible thing about a real broken heart, that you had to carry it around with you and keep living and planning, day to day, in spite of it.

"Yes?" said the maid as she wrenched the door open. By her bleary eyes and the flush of her face, she had probably been dozing by the fire when she was woken by the knock. Hester could see it blazing merrily behind her, its light a small red circle in an otherwise dark room.

"I've a message for Miss Fairbank," Hester said.

"Yes, all right, give it over." When she waited, the maid struggled to right her cap, which was slightly lopsided on her head; her efforts only made it worse. Finally she stared at Hester, who hadn't moved. "Well?"

"It's not a note," Hester said, uncertainly. "It's – I have to tell Miss Fairbank in person."

"Well, you can't see her now. She's gone to bed. And anyway I don't even know who you are or…"

"It's all right, Sarah," a voice from above floated down, and they both looked up to see that Miss Fairbank had unfastened one of the upstairs windows and was leaning out. "I'll be down in a moment."

"Very well, miss," the maid called back with a flabbergasted expression, and she looked Hester over one more time before retreating into the fire-warmed kitchen. She left the door ajar, but since she made no move to invite Hester in, Hester stayed just where she was, in the cold, dark garden. It wasn't even a garden, really, just a dark square of concrete backing onto a high wall. Over the wall, Hester could see the back of another building and, beyond it, the hulking shape of a hydraulic crane.

"You must be Robert's friend, Hester." Miss Fairbank's voice made her jump. The lady had sneaked up behind her almost as quietly as Gentleman Fred. Hester turned around and curtsied, though in her man's coat she probably looked pretty funny doing so.

Miss Fairbank had an Indian shawl wrapped around her head, and with a glance back at the half-open door, she made a gesture for Hester to follow her. They went around the side of the house, pushing open the creaking gate through which Hester had come, and went a little way down the street. Stopping just outside the circle of light thrown by a streetlamp, Miss Fairbank turned back to Hester and leaned in, her voice low and her eyes wide. "I didn't expect to see you so soon. What does Robert say?"

"He'd like to meet you again, miss," Hester said. "He's free after six in the evening tomorrow."

"Hmm." Miss Fairbank's expression was momentarily clouded by indecision, then she said, "I shall be at my aunt's. But perhaps I can slip away for a walk, if he can find his way there. The house is on West Derby Road."

"I've been there before," said Hester. "I can show him." Miss Fairbank's expression cleared.

"Could you? Oh, thank you. But…" She glanced back at her house and adjusted her shawl, which had slipped a little to reveal her golden-brown hair. "The next time you come here, you'd better not call at the servants' door. Tonight we were lucky, as my father is out. But next time, we'd better be careful not to draw too much attention. And servants talk, you know."

Hester could make no reply, as she had been rendered temporarily incapable of speech by a simple phrase of Miss Fairbank's, *next time*, and the fact that she had used that phrase not once, but twice, in the course of a few sentences. It suggested too much, far more than Hester could handle at that moment.

"It would be better to arrange some kind of signal," Miss Fairbank went on. "But we can talk about all that tomorrow evening. I'd better get back. Thank you, Hester." With a final smile and a swish of skirts, she hurried back to the house. Hester watched as she slipped inside the front door and shut it behind her without a sound.

It was too late to report back to Robert now. He was probably still up, but she would wait till morning before giving him Miss Fairbank's answer. At any rate, to return to the bakery at that moment would have been too difficult. By morning, Hester hoped, she would have recovered some strength and settled into her role as a go-between. Miss Fairbank's talk of signals and *next time*s had made it clear that that was what was expected of Hester. So Hester would do it, at least for as long as she could stand to. At the rate things were moving already between Robert and Miss Fairbank, though, it suddenly struck her that maybe her services would not be needed for very long. Maybe it would only take a few agonising months before Robert sat her down one day and told her the news she dreaded to hear, the news that he and Miss Fairbank were…

Hester came around onto Albert Dock before she could finish that thought, and a wall of salty wind stopped her in her tracks for a moment. Mindful of what Gentleman Fred had said, she had taken a different route home through the maze of side-streets behind the docks, one which brought her out at Harold Fairbank's warehouse. Hester had often noticed Fairbank's warehouse before, as it was the newest one on the dock and right beside the Dock Office. Each warehouse on Albert Dock had its own landing stage, so that imported goods could be loaded directly from ships into storage. The windows of Fairbank's warehouse were dark, but as Hester went along, the only sounds around her the slap of water against the landing stages and the creak of the hydraulic cranes, she saw that the lights in Davies's old warehouse, at the other end of the dock, were on. The ship that had been moored by its landing stage was dark, silent, and waiting, just as Gentleman Fred had described. It loomed larger than the other ships in port. Hester wondered where it had come from.

And then, as above her the moon cleared a bank of cloud and illuminated the flag flying from the ship's mizzen gaff, Hester's silent question was answered. The flag was a blue 'X' with white stars on it, against a red background.

"You see it too?" Fred Small materialised from behind an anchor post and Hester nearly fell over in surprise.

"Yes, I see it, and didn't I tell you to stay away from here?"

"Couldn't help it." Fred gazed up at the ship admiringly. "That's a Confederate flag, isn't it?"

"Suppose so."

"Do you suppose it's a warship? Maybe they're smuggling guns and things."

"How am I to know?" said Hester shortly. "Go on, get home now."

"Not yet. I want to take a closer look." Fred darted away before she could get a hold on him. Hester shook her head and, after a moment's hesitation, followed. Coming closer to the old warehouse, she could see that the vast loading doors had been dragged back. She had never seen them open before. There was a metal staircase at the side that led to the upper levels, and that was the way in she had always been used to take. With a thrill of fear, she wondered if whoever was using Davies's warehouse had already found her little hiding place in the loft and disturbed her things.

"Hester!" The hiss came from a few paces ahead. Evidently Fred was too excited at this moment to call her 'Miss Grace' as he usually did. The moon had gone behind another cloud, and Fred was only a dark shape, rendered slightly odd by the boxy shoulders of the frock coat that was too big for him. "Come on!"

She caught up with him near the loading doors and tried to pull him back. "You'll be seen."

"The coast is clear. I've already checked," Fred insisted, and caught hold of her sleeve, dragging her a little further on so that they could see through the loading doors into the interior of the warehouse. Piled in several rows were bales and bales of cotton. Hester stared, blinked, and stared again. She had never seen so much cotton in one place before.

"If we take one –" Fred started to stay, but then the sound of footsteps came from behind them, and Hester acted quickly, dragging herself and Fred into the warehouse and behind the nearest bale of cotton. They threw themselves down on the cold stone floor, trying to quiet their heavy breathing.

"... counted them all?" said a man's voice. It sounded like he had an American accent, although a funny kind of one Hester didn't think she had ever heard before, and living in Albert Dock over the years she had heard many different accents.

"Yes, sir," returned another voice, this one English.

"Good. Then let's close up the place. And remember what Fairbank said. The stuff needs to be out of here first thing tomorrow."

"Yes, sir." The voices grew more distant, and all of a sudden Hester and Fred were plunged into darkness. A moment later there came a terrible groaning sound that seemed to make their very bodies vibrate, but it was only the doors closing.

Fred was clutching Hester's sleeve again and she could hear that he was breathing hard. "It's all right," she muttered to him, and repeated it a few times until she could hear his breathing slow down. She herself had never been afraid of the dark, though she could understand why someone might be. For Hester it had always been the other way around. It was the light of day that she found frightening because it made things inescapable; it forced truths into the open and accepted no compromise.

CHAPTER SEVEN

Hester Grace's little den, in which she'd been staying for more than a year now, had thankfully been undisturbed by the intruders into Davies's warehouse. After the men had shut them into the warehouse, she had shown Fred how to get out by the outer stairs. Then, through the darkness, she felt her way through the old packing rooms and abandoned offices. Her fingers recognised the familiar grooves in the walls, and when the occasional something brushed against her feet, she did not shriek or scream. She was used to sharing this place with the rats. It was better than sharing it with people.

That was why, when her hands found at last the splintery wood of the ladder that led up to the loft, Hester felt the tension flow out of her limbs and the breath crash out of her lungs. She could tell already, just by the feel and smell of the place as she climbed up into it, that no one had been here. When her practised hands found the box of matches and lit one to illuminate her little kingdom, her own corner of the world, she smiled for the first time all day.

There was one window in the loft that was too high up and too small to show anything other than sky, and there was a fishy smell that always lingered over everything, but that was general to Albert Dock. Hester barely noticed it anymore. Her loving eyes saw only the couple of dog-eared books leaning against each other like old friends, a white handkerchief laid out beneath them to cover the bit of driftwood that Hester had fashioned into a shelf, the blanket made from the cheapest kind of wool, devil's dust, but dyed in a very pretty blue and neatly folded on her straw pallet, the yard of calico print that she had nicked from the dressmaker Mrs. Sharp's, which now hung on the wall to give a bit of colour to the place, and whose edges were slightly curled with damp. The whole loft was so small that it hardly afforded her more space than she'd had in the packed girls' dormitory at Brownlow Hill, and when she stood at her full height, her head hit the ceiling. But it was hers, and therefore dear, and dearest of all was the pile of objects in one corner which would, very soon, form themselves in Hester's latest invention: a rusty pair of scissors, a flattened-out piece of tin, a vial of fish glue, and a round piece of cardboard.

She let the match burn out and put it carefully back on the box, feeling her way to the mattress. Since it was a cold night, she kept her coat on as she crawled under the scratchy devil's dust blanket. But while her body was tired, she lay awake for some time, thinking about whether to tell Robert what she had seen and heard tonight. There had to be a mistake or misunderstanding somewhere. Suppose she had misheard the man, or suppose he had been talking about another 'Fairbank'? But then suppose that it was the same Mr. Fairbank, and that he was importing cotton grown by slaves. Didn't Mr. Locksmith have a right to know before he got into a deal with him? He ought to have the facts, at least so that he could make his own investigations and come to his own conclusions. This was what Hester kept coming back to. But then, as soon as she had reached that point in her reasoning, she would feel a stab of guilt, because telling Mr. Locksmith meant telling Robert, and if the deal between Mr. Locksmith and Mr. Fairbank was broken, then whatever was blossoming between Miss Fairbank and Robert might be nipped in the bud, too.

Hester was so exhausted by her own mental back-and-forth that when she got up in the chilly grey dawn, she had only snatched a few hours' sleep. In the bakery, Robert was already up, of course, and judging by the shadows under his eyes it looked like he had not gotten much sleep either. Hester found him in the kitchen, standing by the open door of the oven, the muscles in his upper back straining as he heaved a tray inside.

"Hester!" He stared at her as he shut the door, and then a new eagerness lit in his clear blue eyes. "Did you go to Canning Place last night?"

After a moment, Hester nodded. Robert wiped his brow with the back of his hand and went on, "So how did it – what did she – did you –" Before he could get a complete question out, Cecil's voice called from out in the bakery, "Robert!"

"Sorry," said Robert to Hester. "Just a minute." He sidestepped her to get out. Hester stayed where she was for a minute, the close heat of the place hitting her face in waves. Then she took a breath and went out, too. In the bakery, Cecil Locksmith was dressed in his travelling clothes and had his portmanteau in one hand.

Robert, mid-conversation with Cecil, glanced back over his shoulder at Hester with an expression that, on anyone else, would have been irritation at being interrupted. Robert Burrows's face, though, was too open and amiable to express such sentiments, and so at most the look in his eyes might have been called affectionate impatience. "Cecil's about to get his train," he told her, "so I'm just seeing him off."

"You're Hester, aren't you?" said Mr. Locksmith, quite kindly. Hester nodded, and he smiled at her before looking back at Robert. "Well, if I want to catch the eight o'clock I'd best be off."

"Travel safely," said Robert, shaking his hand. "And congratulations again."

"Don't congratulate me yet! As I said, I never believe a thing until I see it in writing."

"Pardon me," said Hester, finding her voice at last, and they both looked towards her. "But there's something I have to tell you." As Robert opened his mouth, she added firmly, "Both of you."

The clock in the back room of the bakery had struck eight o'clock, but Cecil Locksmith showed no signs of moving from his chair. Instead, he passed his hand up his forehead, over his receding hairline and behind his head to smooth down hair that was already flat. He wasn't a man who had much colour to begin with, but what little colour there was in his face had drained out of it as soon as Hester finished her account.

"Maybe –" Robert began, and they both looked towards him, Cecil with his eyes half-closed in resignation, and Hester with an odd, almost guilty look. Robert went on, thinking hard, "Maybe, times being what they are… I mean, mills are shutting down all over the country and if the only way to keep them open –"

"It's indefensible, Robert," Cecil cut him off. "You know it as well as I. If the cotton coming in keeps workers here employed, that doesn't change the fact that it was grown by slaves."

"But is there really such a difference?" Robert stopped. He could feel Hester's intense gaze on him. Cecil, meanwhile, had his head in his hands. Robert cleared his throat and went on, "I mean, where else is Fairbank supposed to source his cotton? Egypt? India? I don't suppose the workers there are much better off than the slaves in the American South, but we ignore that because we have to, don't we? We have problems in our own country and people starving on our own doorstep and so what difference does it make if we get cotton from an African slave or an Indian worker?"

Cecil said nothing, but Hester said, "One of them is a free man and one isn't."

Robert nodded, the truth of this making him sink into silence.

"You can't reason this away, Robert," Cecil said at last, removing his hands from his face to address his brother-in-law. The pressure of his palms had left red marks on his pale skin. "It's wrong and the whole world knows it's wrong. And everything that Hester has described, everything about the underhand way that this has been carried out, delivering the cotton at night, using Byron Davies's old warehouse, suggests to me that Fairbank knows it's wrong, too. It may not be illegal to import cotton grown by slaves, but if Fairbank wants to be seen as honest and honourable…"

"But it may not even be true." Now Robert could feel that his voice had taken on a pleading tone, and he looked down at the table, half-ashamed. "There may be some misunderstanding."

"I thought so, too," Hester said, "and that's why I wasn't sure I ought to tell you or not."

"No, you did right by telling us, Hester." Cecil gave her a watery smile, and she looked back at him doubtfully. "I shall just have to see Mr. Fairbank as soon as I can, and I'll put off going back to Manchester until I've spoken with him. I hope you won't mind my imposing on your hospitality a little longer, Robert."

"Of course not." Robert pushed back his chair. "But that reminds me, I'd better go open up. I'll tell Marcus to get you something to eat. You, too, Hester. You must be hungry."

Outside, in the cooler air of the bakery, he took a deep breath and let it whistle out through his teeth. Then he went to turn the 'Closed' sign on the door to 'Open', and after that he took out the book-keeping pad from behind the counter and opened it to a new page. Finally he leaned an elbow on the counter, feeling a wave of dizziness come over him as he remembered that he'd had no sleep last night. "Indefensible," he murmured to himself. It was indefensible, what Mr. Fairbank was doing. That was what Cecil had said, which would make any pursuit of Mr. Fairbank's daughter by Robert, at the very least, ill-advised. Of course, she wasn't to blame for her father's business practices, but the instant he thought that, there came unbidden into Robert's mind the memory of what Miss Fairbank had said, about always accompanying her father to meetings and offering him a second opinion. And then he wondered if, assuming that Mr. Fairbank was importing cotton from the Confederate South, his daughter might also be a party to it.

Robert flinched as though he had been struck. No, of course Miss Fairbank was blameless, and he must go on believing her to be. He would think of her just as he had seen her yesterday, lovely, clever, and good. Whatever stain lay on her father's honour, she would still be spotless. Comforted by this new line of thought, Robert straightened, and as the first customer came into his bakery, he was able to greet them with something resembling his usual smile.

CHAPTER EIGHT

I t was always a little troubling to Hester whenever Robert Burrows said or did something to remind her that he was not, in fact, the prince to her little mermaid. These occasions were rare, because most of the time, Robert really was like someone out of a storybook. His smile could cast a spell, his eyes were like the sea on a summer's day, or, at least, they were the kind of blue that Hester imagined to be the blue of the sea on a summer's day, for she had only the River Mersey as a point of reference. He was kind and gracious, too, and almost always cheerful, unless his warm heart made him cast down on someone else's behalf, such as when Alice Smith's husband had died a few years back, or when the bookseller's sick dog had to be put out of his misery last Christmas.

This morning, when they were sitting in the back room discussing what ought to be done about Mr. Fairbank,

Hester had seen a flash of something in Robert. His forehead had pinched together, and the corners of his mouth had drawn down as he started questioning whether there was a difference between importing cotton from the Confederacy or any other part of the world, and for a moment he looked like a different man. For Hester, when news of an American civil war had begun to spread around the docks last spring, the question of who was right and who was wrong had been a simple one. In this war, there was black and white, good and bad, freedom and slavery. Hester had never thought twice before coming down on one side. Her opinion on the war might not have been of much importance to anyone else, but she had one anyway. On the other hand, there was Robert, looking so strange and saying such things that she was forced to wonder, for the first time, whether he really knew or understood as much as she had always given him credit for knowing and understanding.

"You're very quiet," said Cecil Locksmith, and Hester gave a start.

"Sorry, sir, were you saying something?" As Mr. Locksmith was going to Fairbank's offices, he had offered to walk as far as the docks with Hester when he had found out they were going in the same direction, but since they had left the bakery, she had been absorbed in her own thoughts, barely noticing anything around her.

"No, I've been quiet, too." Mr. Locksmith peered up at the overcast sky, before glancing sidelong at her again. "You

60

mustn't worry about your part in this, Hester. I won't say anything to Fairbank about where I got this information, and if there's any misunderstanding, we'll get it straightened out, don't worry."

"I hope it is a misunderstanding," she murmured, and meant it, too, as she recalled the look of excitement in Robert's eyes when she had first come in and he had been about to ask her about Miss Fairbank. Looking towards Davies's warehouse in the distance, she pointed. "The ship's gone, in any case. It was gone when I left this morning at first light."

Cecil followed her gaze and was silent for a moment before shaking his head. Whatever he was thinking, he kept it to himself. They were coming up to Mr. Fairbank's warehouse now, which was teeming with activity as men unloaded silos of grain off what looked like an Irish ship. Cecil stopped and turned to Hester, holding out a hand.

"Well, Hester Grace, if I don't see you before I go back to Manchester, then you'll know it's good news."

Hester shook his hand, too distracted to feel uncertain about a gentleman offering her such a gesture. "But if things go badly, sir…"

"Yes?" Cecil prompted, gently.

She looked up at him. "Then what will happen?"

A flock of seagulls that had settled on the dome of the Dock Office chose that moment to burst into noisy flight, and Mr. Locksmith had to raise his voice to be heard over their racket. "I'll break my deal with Mr. Fairbank, of course." His face took on that same look of resignation that he'd had back in the bakery. "And then I suppose I'll have to look elsewhere for cotton."

"And what will Robert do?" Hester pressed.

"Robert?" Cecil repeated, frowning down at her as though he was not sure whether he had heard right. "It doesn't really concern him one way or the other." Hester looked away quickly, perhaps too quickly, and he went on, "But evidently you don't agree?"

Now she was caught. "I just mean, I'm sure Robert will be happier if your deal comes off."

"Because of Mr. Fairbank's pretty young daughter?" Cecil said, cannily, and Hester looked back at him, startled. "So you know something of this. Perhaps he asked you to send a message or something of that nature?"

"Nothing like that, sir," she lied, feeling her face warm. "He just mentioned her once or twice, that's all, and it made me wonder."

"He's mentioned her more than once or twice to me. In fact, this morning before you came, he could talk of nothing else. It's plain enough to see what's going on." An indulgent smile had formed on Cecil's thin lips, but then the smile seemed to freeze as he looked back at Fairbank's warehouse. Hester followed his gaze, thinking he must have seen something to alarm him, but there was nothing out of the ordinary that she could see, only the same men hauling silos into the warehouse, and loading whatever they didn't bring into the warehouse onto the back of a waiting cart, whose horses tripped back and forth over the stony, uneven ground. Cecil, watching the activity, said, "Whether the deal comes off or not, whether I continue to work with Mr. Fairbank, it's the least of Robert's worries, if he's set his sights on Miss Simona."

"You don't think she likes him back?" said Hester, who could not hide her surprise at the idea.

"She might very well 'like him back', as you say. It wouldn't make much difference. I doubt Mr. Fairbank would want a baker for a son-in-law."

Hester didn't know what to say to that. Seeming to notice her silence, Cecil glanced back at her. "Don't think me a snob. I married a mill worker from Vauxhall, but then I wasn't much better off myself when Lesley and I first met. I was a clerk. Miss Fairbank is a merchant's daughter, and Harold Fairbank is not just any merchant. Robert is a baker. There is a difference, unfortunately, these days more than ever."

He lingered a moment more, as though there was something else he wanted to say, though he didn't seem to know what. He just stood, hands in his coat pockets, looking her up and down in a considering way. Hester, sensing the new atmosphere and not sure whether she liked it or not, said hastily, "You'd better not delay any longer, sir. I'm sure Mr. Fairbank is a very busy man."

"Yes," said Cecil with a sigh, "and it will be no easy task getting hold of him, I can sense. Good day." They shook hands once again, but this time Hester did not meet Cecil's gaze. She curtsied and got away as quickly as she could. It wasn't the first time in her life that a man had looked at her like that, and she did not dwell on the moment for too long. Her mind was more occupied in going over Cecil's words about Robert, which had forced upon her the second surprising conclusion of the day. Not only did Robert not always behave like a prince, it seemed, but there were actually people walking this earth who had never seen him as such to begin with, who seemed to see him as just ordinary, too ordinary, even.

CHAPTER NINE

Hester was hopelessly behind on her invention, which she had hoped to have finished today so that she could bring it to Cronshaw's and see what she could get for it. Most pawnbrokers in town wouldn't have had any interest in whatever contraptions Hester could cook up, but she had been going to Harry Cronshaw for years and he was fond of her. He might give her three shillings for this, which would last her a nice while if she could stretch it out.

As soon as Hester returned to her den, therefore, she cast Robert and Cecil and the Fairbanks out of her mind and got down to work. She was glad she had eaten something at the bakery, because now her hands were steady and her brain was ticking over, and for a few hours at least she wouldn't have to think about how she was going to get her next meal.

She had barely been working a quarter of an hour, though, when something made her look up, and she saw that the top rung of the ladder which led into the loft was shaking, as though under someone's weight. Whoever they were, they were moving very quietly. Hester found a rock in the pocket of her overcoat and shot to her feet, nearly hitting her head on the ceiling, but she managed to keep her voice calm as she called out, "Who's there?"

The ladder went still, and an agonising few seconds passed before a familiar voice called up to her, "I beg your pardon, Miss Grace, but I thought you were out."

Hester let out a breath, and then stalked over to the ladder, reaching down and seizing Gentleman Fred by the collar of his frock coat. "Get in." She dragged him up the rest of the way, ignoring his protests, and let him go all at once so that he stumbled and nearly knocked down her books. "Have you brought anyone else?"

"No one, Miss Grace," Fred panted, struggling back to his feet, "I give you my word."

"Your word isn't worth much to me. How do you find this place? I suppose you followed me."

"If I'd followed you, then I'd know you were home, wouldn't I?" Fred retorted, before checking himself. "Forgive me. That was ungentleman-like. But perhaps, Miss Grace, if you didn't manhandle me every time we met..."

"Answer my question," she interrupted, and Fred sighed. This time he was wearing a top hat and seemed to want to draw attention to the fact as he took it off and held it in front of him.

"It wasn't difficult to find, Miss Grace. It was just a matter of retracing my steps to the entrance that you showed me last night and, after that, nothing more than common sense."

"I knew I shouldn't have shown you." Hester muttered, but didn't bother to finish her sentence. "And why did you come when you thought I wasn't home? I've nothing here worth stealing, you know."

"I wouldn't exactly say that," Fred said mysteriously, but as she opened her mouth to interrupt, he hurried on, "So many questions, Miss Grace! May I ask one now? Who was that gentleman you were talking with, over by the Dock Office?"

"None of your business," said Hester. "And I thought you said you weren't following me."

"I wasn't! I happened to be passing a half hour ago and it drew my attention. Have you friends in high places, Miss Grace?"

"I've told you it's none of your business," Hester said. "Now, are you going to tell me why you're here or will I have to use this?" She opened her fist to show him the rock that she was still holding, and Fred feigned shock.

"Really, between friends…–"

"Small!"

"Very well, very well. I am here at the behest of Billy Ross."

Hester sighed. "Why doesn't that surprise me?"

"But I didn't lie to you last night, Miss Grace," Fred said hastily, "when I said I no longer worked for Mr. Ross or any of his compatriots. That was true at the time. However…"

"However?"

"Well, since you had no interest in my business proposition I was forced to return to the fold."

Hester stared at him in utter bewilderment. "Business proposition?"

Fred sighed. "Might I sit, Miss Grace, and rest my weary legs?" At her grudging nod, he unbuttoned his frock coat and then sat cross-legged, showing up the scuffed soles of his otherwise clean boots. Hester sat, too, on her pallet, arranging the devil's dust blanket under her.

"You'll recall," Fred said once he had made himself comfortable, "that when we saw those bales of cotton downstairs, I proposed taking one? Well, it seemed too good an opportunity to pass up, and one, too, which afforded no time for reflection. So I went to Mr. Ross, told him what we had found, and the two of us returned here last night."

"You didn't," Hester exclaimed. "Tell me you didn't –"

"We only took one bale. No one will even notice it's gone."

"You don't think they've counted them? Small, what were you thinking?"

"I was thinking," said Fred calmly, "that an opportunity had presented itself, and that I would have to act quickly to benefit from it. And it's a good thing I did act quickly, because when I returned this morning all the cotton was gone."

"Aye." Hester spoke in a low voice. "They took it away before first light." She glanced up at Fred, warily. "I suppose you probably got away with it. This time. But it was a risk."

"We deal in risks, like any other men of business."

Hester shook her head and laughed. Fred, leaning his elbows on his knees, didn't seem offended by her response. His eyes, eager and interested, had passed her to regard the contraption in the corner of the loft. "Might I take a closer look?"

"It's not finished." Hester began, but then her own eagerness overcame her and she got up, gesturing for Fred to come by her side. It was rare enough, after all, that she got to show her inventions to anyone, even Robert, who took a lively interest but had, of course, never had cause to come up here. "It's a simple thing, really. I got the idea from something I saw when I worked in a dressmaker's a few years back. It's a steam-powered fan."

"Steam-powered," Fred repeated solemnly, with a nod as his eyes ran over the various bits of machinery.

"Yes. So this piece of cardboard I cut from a match box, and see, I cut along the edges of the circle, too, the what-do-you-call-it? And then, this bit of tin here, I had to heat it to get it nice and flat…"

"Where did you do that? You couldn't have a fire here."

"A friend let me use his," said Hester after a moment.

"Your gentleman friend?" said Fred, and she rolled her eyes without replying.

"Anyway, I glued the tin to the cardboard and this part will be the rotor of the fan. I still have to finish the boiler, but then once I've lit the candle underneath, here, the water in the boiler will heat and turn to steam and that will power the fan."

Hester had been talking faster and faster in her excitement, and now that she had finished, she turned to Fred to see his reaction. He just looked blankly at her.

"How do you think of these things?"

"I don't know," said Hester, stumped by the question. "I've always liked seeing how things work. Taking them apart, putting them back together. I used to do it back in Brownlow Hill…" She shut up her mouth, because she didn't like talking about the workhouse, especially with someone she knew she couldn't trust. With a sidelong glance to Fred, she said, "Anyway. Tell me why you've come."

Fred, who had crouched down to look at the fan, got to his feet now and stretched. He was short enough that his head did not hit the ceiling. Hester stood, too, and he looked up at her with an expression that was suddenly knowing. "Like I said, Billy Ross sent me. He's interested in you."

"Tell him I'm not interesting," Hester said, keeping her voice even as her heartbeat picked up its pace.

"I've tried, believe me. But he's heard you're clever with these things. He sent me to see if I could figure out what kind of material you use for your inventions, and how you do it."

"Why?"

"Why else? Because he thinks it would be a good way of making money."

"I make nothing from this stuff," Hester said, gesturing to the fan. "Barely enough to live on."

"But you'd make more if you joined us."

Hester stared at Fred. "You know I can't do that. You know I'd never join Billy Ross's gang."

"I know." Fred's voice dropped. "But I'm afraid he doesn't see any reason why not. And he thinks you ought to know that things might get harder for you, if you continue working here on your own."

Hester thought this over for a minute, and then took hold of Fred by the sleeve of his coat, moving him towards the ladder. "Well. You can tell him that I've been on this patch longer than him, or you, and I'm not about to be scared off it by some kids. And you can tell him that if he has a bone to pick with me, he can come here and do it himself instead of sending a messenger."

Fred's doubtful face looked up at her from the ladder. "You sure you want me to say all that?"

"What else is there to say?" Hester returned, flatly. "Go on, get out." She waited by the ladder until it stopped shaking, and she listened hard for the sound of Fred Small's retreating footsteps. Only when those had faded away did she take a deep breath, putting her hands to her head and pushing up her hair before letting it fall loose again. Her heart was still hammering in her chest. When she tried to get back to work, she found that her heartbeat would not slow down, nor would her hands stop shaking. Billy Ross's threats fresh in her mind, she got up, put on her overcoat, and set out from the warehouse.

CHAPTER TEN

R obert had a bad day of it. He wasn't sure if he had ever had a worse day, in fact, even as an apprentice, because at least back then he had been eager and willing to learn. Today, though, his mind would focus on nothing, swinging wildly between Cecil and Hester and the Fairbanks to his own lack of sleep, and never able to do more than register the words of his customers. At first people were patient and smiling, but as the queue in the bakery got longer and longer, and the windows fogged up with condensation, and Robert gave the wrong change here and the wrong order there, the general mood became more querulous. Marcus came out from behind the counter and started running around trying to smooth things over. Marcus, smoothing things over! That should have been indication enough to Robert that something was seriously wrong, while several people ended up walking out saying that they would take their custom elsewhere.

Even this did not have the effect on Robert that it ought to have had. Normally he would have borne up, fought it out for the last few hours and kept a smile fixed on his face no matter how crabby his customers became. Now he just felt ready to give in. At half-past five when the shop bell rang and he saw, at last, Cecil walk in looking as weary as he felt, Robert told Marcus to serve the last customer and then close up shop.

"Now, Mr. Burrows?"

"Yes, now. We'll close a half-hour early today."

Without waiting for his apprentice's response, Robert took off his apron and followed Cecil inside to the back room. "Well?"

"I've had quite a day," Cecil said over his shoulder. "It took hours before Fairbank would even meet me."

"And then?" Robert said eagerly. He watched as Cecil made for the stairs that led up to his room. "Where are you going?"

"To fetch my bag. I'm getting the six o'clock train to Manchester, if I can make it on time."

Robert felt a great weight lift from his shoulders. "Then the deal's back on?" he called up hopefully as Cecil climbed the stairs.

"I think so," Cecil called back, and Robert murmured a small prayer of thanksgiving under his breath.

"That's very good news."

Cecil came clattering back down the stairs with his portmanteau in hand and looked at his brother-in-law strangely as he descended. "Aren't you going to ask me what Fairbank said?"

"Well," said Robert, a little confusedly, "I suppose it was all a misunderstanding, wasn't it?"

"It seems so, yes." Cecil walked on and Robert followed him through to the bakery, which was empty now but for Marcus. "He gave me his word, at least."

"Well, that ought to be good enough for anyone." Robert looked over his shoulder at his apprentice. "Marcus, I'm walking Mr. Locksmith to Lime Street Station. Will you lock up?"

"Yes, Mr. Burrows," his apprentice called back, and Robert went on, nearly stepping on Cecil's heels as they came out on Cobbler's Lane.

"We'd better step it up if you want to make it for six o'clock."

"Don't you need a coat?" Cecil said, looking Robert up and down, but the latter shrugged.

"It's not too cold this evening. Go on, tell me what else Fairbank said. Was he angry?"

"At first, perhaps." Cecil paused. "But then I explained the circumstances, without mentioning Hester directly, of course, and he agreed that it looked strange. He told me that the warehouse is still occasionally used by Davies even though most of his mills have closed down, so perhaps the men Hester saw last night were employed by Davies or one of his business partners. And he thinks, Fairbank, that is, that it can't have been a Confederate ship. He says the Union blockade is so strong that no Confederate ship could possibly make it across the Atlantic with her cargo intact. I confess I thought the same thing when Hester told us that."

"Me, too," Robert said. "Though I didn't like to say it in front of her. But she must have been mistaken."

"And as for the name…" They had reached the top of Cobbler's Lane now, and Cecil paused again, looking down as they turned onto Dale Street. "Well, when I got to that part of the story, he actually started laughing. He reminded me that 'Fairbank' is a very common name, especially in this part of the country. I felt a bit foolish after that."

"'Fairbank' is a common name," Robert agreed. But a lovely one, he added, silently. His mind was opening, once more, to so many joyous possibilities that he felt rather dizzy.

"So on the whole, I don't think he was really offended," Cecil went on, "though I suppose that remains to be seen. I hope this won't sour things down the line."

"I'm sorry," Robert said, after a moment. "It looks like Hester let her imagination get away from her."

"She thought she was doing right," Cecil responded, and then he fixed Robert with another strange look. "Don't be too hard on her."

"Of course not!"

"I just mean…" They turned onto Old Haymarket and Cecil checked his pocket watch before picking up his pace. "Well, she reminds me a little of your sister."

"Of Lesley?" Robert exclaimed.

"Not Lesley as she is now, perhaps, but how she was when we first met. When she was working in Wilson's mill, and I was a clerk. I used to see her walking into the mill in the mornings, all alone, all her sorrows and hardships written on her face, and yet, if I had tried to help her in those days, she would have scorned me. There was something about her, a curtain that I couldn't lift." Cecil's voice had softened in tenderness, making Robert glance towards him curiously. His brother-in-law went on, in the same tone, "Hester reminds me of that."

"She can certainly take care of herself," Robert said after a moment's hesitation. "If that's what you mean."

"It isn't. Not really." Cecil sighed. "Hester has never asked you for help, has she?"

"I do what I can for her, but…"

"But she's never asked. Has she?"

"No." Robert uttered the word with a little surprise. "No, I suppose she hasn't."

"I thought not. That doesn't mean she doesn't need it, however. But I'm sure, as you say, that you do what you can." Cecil frowned and did not say any more, as they were nearly at Lime Street station. Had Robert's mind not been so distracted, he might have dwelt on the conversation for longer than the few minutes it took to see Cecil onto the platform.

CHAPTER ELEVEN

The front door of the bakery was locked when Hester got to it, which surprised her as it was only quarter past six. She dithered around for a minute, peering in the dark windows, and was about to go around to check the back when someone called,

"He's closed up early."

Hester looked up to the street to where the bookseller, Mr. Moss, was standing with his arms folded over his chest. She wondered how long he had been watching her. Nodding her head in acknowledgement of what he had said, she averted her gaze, but he carried on, "Sent the young boy off, too. I saw him heading home a half hour ago. Rather strange, if you ask me."

Hester hadn't asked, had no intention of asking in fact, but her lack of response only seemed to make the old man more eager to talk. "I went in there for my scones earlier, always do on a Wednesday, and he gave me fruit instead of plain. I didn't say anything seeing as he charged me the same. But there's something on that young man's mind, that's for sure."

Hester nodded and began to move away. "Well, good evening."

"Not so fast! Come back here." She turned back to see the bookseller crooking his finger at her. Sighing, Hester made her way up the street to the bookstand. The books had all been brought inside, leaving only an empty table, over which Mr. Moss put a loving hand as he said with faint reproach, "You knocked over my *Tristram Shandy* yesterday, you know."

"Did I? I'm sorry."

"You were in an awful hurry somewhere, looks like. Something on your mind too, perhaps?" The bookseller looked at her hard. "Where's your coat?"

"It was stolen," Hester said. That was a lie. She had actually given it to a man on the Scotland Road earlier today, in exchange for the knife which she now carried in the pocket of her fustian trousers. If Billy Ross had started making threats, then she was going to arm herself as best she could.

"You need a coat," Mr. Moss said, frowning so deeply that his face looked like a wrinkled apple. "It'll be winter soon." Then, without another word, he turned and walked into the draper's shop which was behind the bookstand. Hester saw him descending the stairs to his cellar lodgings, and wondered if he had forgotten about her, if she could just walk away. But then out he came again, bearing in his hand a musty-looking evening coat that looked like it hadn't been worn in forty years. He thrust it at Hester. "Here."

"I don't have any money." she started to say.

"I don't want money, girl. I don't wear it anymore, so someone should get some use out of it."

Hester shook out the coat. With its cinched waist and high, wide lapels, she'd look as funny as Gentleman Fred wearing it, but by the feel of it, it was made from good wool, not that cheap devil's dust stuff she was used to. "Thank you," she said to Mr. Moss, who grunted. Hester slipped on the coat, which felt itchy on her skin and, when she checked her reflection in the window of the draper's shop, made her look about as funny as she'd expected.

"What's your name, girl?" the bookseller asked. Hester told him, and he repeated it to himself a few times as though committing it to memory.

"Hester Grace, Hester Grace. Can you read, Hester Grace?"

"Yes, I can read," she said, a little put out by the question. "I went to school."

"Well, good. Maybe next time you come, I'll have something for you."

She was about to tell him she didn't have time to read books, but then a thought struck her. "Do you have the one about the little mermaid?" she blurted before she could help herself.

Mr. Moss frowned. "What? A little mermaid, you say?"

"Never mind," said Hester quickly. "It's just a story I read once."

"Who wrote it? You don't remember?"

"I don't remember any of it," Hester lied. "Only that I liked it." The bookseller was still looking at her. She could sense his thoughtful gaze even as she kept her eyes averted, wishing they were talking about anything else.

"Well," said Mr. Moss at length, "finding that would be like looking for a needle in a haystack, you understand. But I will do my best."

"You don't have to –" Hester stopped herself, stuffing her hands in the pockets of her coat. Kindness always had this effect on her, especially when she had not been looking for it. It made her feel embarrassed and uncertain. "I'll go and wait for Robert now."

"You might be waiting a long time," Mr. Moss called after her as she started walking for the bakery.

"Yes," Hester called back over her shoulder. "Thank you."

CHAPTER TWELVE

Hester was sitting on the doorstep of the bakery when Robert got back. He had gone for a long walk around town after seeing Cecil off at the station, and his first question when he saw her was, "What time is it?"

"About quarter past eight," she replied straight away without checking anything. Hester was like that; she had an inbuilt clock, whose accuracy Robert had long since stopped questioning.

"That late?" He gave a low whistle as he rummaged for his keys. "You shouldn't have waited for so long. You might have caught a chill."

"I wanted to see you," Hester said, and the softness of her tone, the unusual directness of her words, might have given Robert pause, had he not that moment been caught up in contemplating his own stupidity.

"Hester," he said, giving up the search. "You won't believe this, but I haven't got my keys. I must have forgotten them in my coat, and I left my coat inside. Would you mind?"

Hester had already scrambled up from the doorstep and was making her way around to the back door of the bakery. There was a small window beside it that had been left ajar, through which Robert's broad shoulders would never have fit. Hester, for her part, could just about make it, though she had to take off her coat first, and when she had wriggled through, she landed on the other side with a distinct thump, which made Robert wince.

"Are you hurt?" he called.

"I'm all right," she called back from the darkness, and then the darkness scattered as she lit the oil lamp. A moment later, there came the sound of her unlatching the back door from the inside. Robert, who was holding her coat, looked down at it in confusion, turning it over to examine the lapels and the frocked hem.

"What happened to your good coat?" he asked Hester when she opened the door.

She looked surprised by the question. "I had to sell it."

Robert considered this as he stepped inside. He handed Hester back her coat and then rubbed a hand over his stubbled chin. (Besides having had no sleep, he hadn't remembered to shave either). "Hester…"

"Yes?"

"You know that if you're ever in any kind of trouble, all you have to do is ask," Robert said, "and I'll help you. That is, I'll do what I can. Which might not be much, but I'll certainly do my best."

There was a silence. Hester stared at Robert, the expression in her brown eyes either fearful or hopeful, he couldn't tell which it was until she spoke. "I'm not in trouble. Who told you I was in trouble?"

"No one," Robert said at once. "No one, I didn't mean – Cecil just said earlier that I ought to look out for you, that's all."

"Mr. Locksmith is very kind." Hester's voice was so flat that the words did not seem to have any meaning at all. She had turned to fiddle with the oil lamp so that Robert could not see her expression. "Has he gone back to Manchester?"

"Yes."

"Then I suppose the deal came off?"

As she seemed anxious to change the subject, Robert allowed it. "Yes, he went to Mr. Fairbank, and they talked it over. It looks like you were mistaken in what you saw. No Confederate ship could make it through the Union blockade, anyway. But Cecil doesn't blame you at all, and nor do I. You were right to tell us, and to make sure."

Hester turned then and held up the oil lamp. "This is smoking a bit. Do you want me to see if I can fix it?"

"It doesn't matter," said Robert, as gently as he could. "Thank you, but – but, Hester, you know I've been longing to see you all day. You know, you must know, that I've been longing to hear what Miss Fairbank said to you."

Hester put down the oil lamp, so that there was no longer a screen between their faces. He searched hers desperately now, and thought that he read, in her tightening lips and lowered eyes, his answer. A short, sharp sigh escaped him, and on his next inhalation he said, "You must tell me. You mustn't try to soften the blow. If she's said she won't see me again –"

"She will see you again," Hester said, and Robert sighed again, this time in blessed relief. "In fact, she said you might drop by her aunt's house on West Derby Road this evening after you had finished work, though I think it's too late now for you to go."

"This evening! After work!" All of a sudden, Robert was seized by a new kind of agony. He began to pace up and down. The back room did not leave him much space in which to do that, meaning that Hester had to scuttle out of his way, but he barely noticed or cared. All he could think about were the two hours that he had wasted in pointless wandering after seeing Cecil off to the station, hours which he might have used to see Miss Fairbank. He turned to Hester. "Why didn't you tell me this before?"

"I didn't get the chance!" Hester exclaimed, from the corner to which she had retreated. This time, it didn't take so much to figure out that the look in her eyes, as she regarded Robert, was fearful. "And I thought after what I saw and what we talked about, that maybe you wouldn't want to see Miss Fairbank, at least until you could be sure that her father wasn't mixed up in..."

"Of course I would still want to see her! Never mind what her father does or doesn't do with his business, it makes no difference to me. I don't care –" Robert stopped short, suddenly hearing his own furious voice in his ears like that of a stranger. He collapsed into the nearest chair and covered his face with his hands.

A minute or two passed, judging by the ticks in the clock, though Robert's fevered brain probably wasn't counting them right. But then, a hand came to rest on his shoulder, very lightly, and Hester said, from somewhere behind him, "You don't mean that."

"No," Robert agreed, his voice muffled by his hands. "No, I don't."

"You haven't slept. You're not thinking. But I know you, and I know you care about right and wrong."

"I do." Robert dragged his hands off his face and stared up at her. "Hester, what's happening to me? I feel like I'm going mad. And to think that she was waiting for me tonight, and that I didn't show up, and that she might think me careless or indifferent, that makes me feel madder than anything else."

Hester's hand had tightened a fraction on his shoulder as she spoke, and she was silent for a moment before saying, "It will pass. You'll still feel what you feel, maybe, but the... the madness you're talking of – it will pass."

"I hope so," Robert said miserably. "I don't see how I'm supposed to spend the rest of my life like this. Hester," He reached up to take hold of the hand on his shoulder and clasped it in both of his own as he turned around to face her. She stared down at him. "Hester, could you go to Canning Place and see if you can see her? She must be back from her aunt's by now. Even if you could just see her for a minute, – if you could just tell her that I'm sorry, that it was a misunderstanding..."

Hester withdrew her hand from his and looked away, but after a moment, nodded. Robert sagged in his chair, feeling the relief wash over his limbs in a wave of warmth. It was only a brief reprieve, he knew. Before long he would be agonising about Miss Fairbank's next message to him, about whether or not she would accept his apology. But he would enjoy this calm while it lasted, and perhaps he might even get some sleep tonight.

It was the first time that she had touched him properly. She had done it without thinking because he looked so frightened and desperate. Afterwards, she was afraid that he would turn around and ask her what she was doing, but instead, he had not only accepted her touch but returned it with one of his own. He held her hand in both of his, and looked up into her face, and with those warm blue eyes fixed on her, Hester was surprised she had managed to stay standing. Robert had never looked at her like that before. He had never needed her, she realised as she made her way to Canning Place, as much as he needed her at that moment.

Remembering Miss Fairbank's warning, Hester went around to the back of the house but did not call at the servants' door. Instead she waited in the garden, lingering in the shadows, and fixed her eyes on the windows above, trying to remember which one Miss Fairbank had leaned out of last time. One of them was lighted but the curtains were closed, and from time to time a silhouette would pass across it. Hester thought about throwing a stone but decided against it, as she could not know for sure whether the window belonged to Miss Fairbank's room. She couldn't even tell if the silhouette belonged to Miss Fairbank herself or to one of the servants. So Hester waited, and kept her eyes trained on the lighted window, as the shadows around her deepened and the sky above went from dark blue to black.

About two hours must have passed when the window finally opened and Miss Fairbank leaned out, her eyes scanning the garden and one hand at her white throat. By then the cold had settled into Hester's bones, but she lost no time in stepping forward and calling in a carrying whisper, "Miss! Miss?"

Miss Fairbank gave a start when she saw Hester below and pressed a finger to her lips. She disappeared from the window and reappeared a few minutes later at the back door, in the same manner as she had done before, with the same shawl wrapped around her head. She closed the door very softly behind her before rushing forward to meet Hester.

"Well done!" she said breathlessly. "I was worried you might call at the door again, and Father's home tonight and he would surely have noticed or heard something. Nothing escapes him. No, no it's all right." Hester had begun to move towards the side passage that led to the street. "We can talk here this time since the servants haven't seen you. I can't stay here long, of course. What does he say?"

Quickly, Hester explained that Robert hadn't had the chance to meet Miss Fairbank at West Derby Road earlier and passed on his apologies. When she had finished, Miss Fairbank looked radiant and relieved, just as Robert had done earlier when Hester had told him that Miss Fairbank did indeed want to meet him again.

"Well," Miss Fairbank whispered, "I'm so glad you've come. I really didn't know what to think. I waited ever so long at Aunt Ada's house. I kept making excuses not to leave. I'm sure she was quite bewildered by the end. I only got home a half-hour ago." She paused to draw breath and then went on. "If Robert wants to meet tomorrow, tell him I will be in the Botanic .Gardens all afternoon. Maybe he can get away during his dinner hour. My aunt will be with me, but she always gets tired after half an hour and lets me explore the walks by myself."

"I'll tell him," said Hester, and Miss Fairbank beamed.

"Thank you! Thank you! Goodnight!"

She tiptoed back into the house, easing the door shut behind her, and a minute later Hester looked up and saw a silhouette pass the lighted window. The light winked out, and Hester, blinking, suddenly felt very tired.

On the way home, she bought a bowl of broth for tuppence in one of the beerhouses that lined Albert Dock. She ate quickly, not just because she was hungry but because all around, at every table, there were men watching her. She kept one hand on the knife in her pocket and sat at the very edge of her seat, ready to spring up at the slightest sign of trouble.

Outside, she ran headlong into Gentleman Fred and they both went crashing to the pavement. A man standing in the doorway started laughing, evidently thinking the two of them were drunk. Ignoring him, Hester picked herself up and glared at Fred. "Were you following me again?"

"No, indeed, I give you my word! But one of my compatriots said that they saw you here some minutes ago. And I must confess, I have been looking for you everywhere." Fred got to his feet, shaking his head. "Where have you been?"

"I was busy," Hester said slowly. Her eyes narrowed as they fixed on him. "Why were you looking for me? What's happened?"

Fred glanced towards the man in the doorway and then jerked his head on. He and Hester walked on down the dock, avoiding the groups of sailors and workmen by sticking close to the landing stages, even though at times the water slopped up over the sides and got their feet wet. Fred had no hat on, and as he reached up to mop his brow, Hester could see that his thin frame was trembling very slightly.

"Billy Ross has been arrested," he told her.

"What? How?"

"The police raided our den earlier today. They found the cotton, too, and traced it back to the shipment that landed in Davies's last night."

"Told you they'd notice it was gone."

"I can assure you that they did not! It was only on account of the raid that they found the cotton at all. And after they had done so, they informed Mr. Fairbank and..."

"It wasn't Mr. Fairbank's cotton that you and I saw, last night," Hester corrected him.

"Was it not? I recalled one of those men in the warehouse saying his name. In any case," Fred waved this detail away with a long-fingered, skinny hand, " whoever did own that cotton, the police must have told him, because several men came to Davies's a few hours ago and they have been there ever since, posted outside the entrances. Perhaps another shipment is expected. I must say these men had rather a grim aspect when I saw them."

Hester had stopped dead. Fred walked on for a bit before he noticed she wasn't beside him, and he doubled back. Hester's eyes were fixed on Davies's warehouse, which was now in sight and whose windows, like last night, were once more flooded with light. No ship waited by its landing stage this time, but her heart had sunk all the same at the sight.

"My things," she said quietly. "What if they go up to the loft and find all my things?"

"I assure you they won't," said Fred at once. "Why should they? I only had the good fortune of finding your hiding place because I was searching for it."

Hester did not move from her spot, did not drag her eyes away from the warehouse. Fred went on, jostling her elbow, "These men will have left by morning, I am sure. In the meantime, you merely have to find somewhere else to sleep. Have you anywhere in mind?"

Hester was about to answer that no, of course she didn't, but then she remembered what Robert had said earlier, about what she was to do if she was ever in trouble. She didn't like to bother him, but it wasn't as if a visit to him now would be entirely unwelcome since it would bring him news of Miss Fairbank, too. She looked around and down at Fred and nodded.

"Very good," said Fred, and as she turned and started walking back in the direction in which they had come, he hurried along on her heels. "If I might hazard a guess, is it the bakery on Cobbler's Lane?"

"What do you know about it?" Hester muttered.

"Nothing, of course, but I have noticed its young proprietor from time to time as I happened to be passing by. And from what I have observed, on those occasions when I have seen the two of you together, you appear to be rather struck with him."

Hester started to walk faster. Fred tripped along beside her. "So, this baker of yours would be happy to offer you a place to stay for the night? I daresay he has a soft spot for you."

"He has nothing for me," Hester said through gritted teeth. "He has a kind heart, that's all."

"Then it will be all the same to him if I come along, too?"

It took Hester a minute to realise what Fred was asking. Then she stared down at him in incredulity and shook her head. "Not a chance."

"Now, Miss Grace, be reasonable. I have nowhere else to go. At this moment I am utterly destitute and friendless in this world. I cannot return to our den, as it has been compromised. I barely escaped last time, and with Billy Ross and most of the boys in Seel Street station, I imagine it is only a matter of time before the police track me down, too. I simply need somewhere to stay for the night, and in the morning, I can make plans."

"I'm not bringing you to Robert's place," said Hester. "I hardly feel right about going there myself, never mind bringing someone else."

They had passed from Albert Dock into Canning Dock by now, and Hester turned away from the river to make for the side-street that led to Canning Place and thence to Cobbler's Lane. Fred was still following her. For a moment, there was no sound except for the slap of their bare feet against the wet ground. Then Fred said again, in a voice more forlorn and pathetic than any she had heard him use before, "Please, Hester."

Hester was silent until they came onto the street, drawing away from the docks, away from the cruel wind and the incessant noise of revellers. Finally she turned to Fred, forcing him to halt. She spoke more gently than she was accustomed to doing with him. "I'd help you if I could, Small, but I can't bring you to Robert's. He's kind, but I can't push him that far. I don't..." She swallowed, and the next words came out unbidden. They felt like they were being pulled from somewhere deep inside her. "I don't know what would happen if I did."

Fred Small nodded, thrusting his hands into the pockets of his coat and not meeting her gaze as he murmured, "Goodnight, then." He walked back towards the docks, and Hester walked on towards the safety of Robert's bakery, doing her best to shake off the encounter.

CHAPTER THIRTEEN

The clean and sweet scent of baking bread greeted Hester when she awoke the next morning, after the soundest sleep that she had enjoyed in a long time, but it was not the smell that had awoken her. It was Robert's hand on her shoulder, as he knelt by the settee in the back room where she had put up for the night. For a few seconds, as Hester blinked up into his dear, friendly face, she was breathless with happiness. Then Robert said, sounding uncertain, "There's someone out front for you."

He got up and went into the kitchen. Hester saw by the clock above the door that it was just gone seven. She sat up, dislodging the blanket that had been draped over her knees, and saw, looking down at herself, that Robert's hand had left a faint, floury imprint on the shoulder of her shirt. She put her own hand over it for a moment. Then she got up, taking her coat from the hook on which

Robert had hung it last night, and went out into the bakery.

The displays were all set up, though the 'Open' sign on the door was still facing inward. Marcus, Robert's apprentice, was peering out through the windows at a boy who was standing outside, a boy with a bruised face, who was clutching something in his hands that looked like an old sack. As Hester approached the door, Marcus turned and asked, with the same uncertainty in his voice as there had been in Robert's, "Do you know him?"

"Aye," said Hester. "I know him." She passed out the door and into the raw morning air, coming up to Fred. "What is it? What's happened to you?"

There was a strange look in Fred Small's eyes. Even though he was the one who was pale as death and covered in bruises, he looked sorry for her. When he passed her what he had been holding, Hester understood why. Wrapped up in the length of calico that had hung on her wall were a bit of tin with cardboard glued onto it, a pair of scissors and the stub of a candle.

"I'm afraid it was all I could save," Fred said, in a voice that was shot through with exhaustion and fear. "They took the rest of it, said it had been stolen."

Hester shook her head as she turned over the objects in her hands. Her own few, precious treasures, stolen? Who would she have stolen them from? And, more to the point, "Who's they?" She looked back up at Fred, reached out a hand but drew it back again before it could touch his face. "The ones who did this to you?"

Fred nodded without meeting her gaze. "But I am to blame," he said. "I shouldn't have gone back there. I thought I could sneak past the men at the door and stay in the loft for the night. I know." For Hester had drawn herself up to her full height, ready to explode at him. "I'm well aware of my own foolishness in this, Miss Grace! I couldn't think of where else to go. And I didn't think that these men had seen me sneaking in. I didn't imagine that they'd follow me. When they found me up in the loft, they thought I must have come back to steal more cotton and hide it there, and they tore around your place looking for it. When they didn't find anything, they said they would teach me a lesson instead."

"You led them right there? To my place?" Hester knew that she ought to be asking another question. She ought to be asking if Fred was hurt anywhere else, how he had gotten away from the men, if he was still in danger, but a deep cold was spreading through her, passing down the length of her spine, settling in her stomach.

"I know," said Fred Small again. "I am sorry. I had nowhere else to go."

"That's not my fault." Hester was made of ice now, and her words came out brittle and hard. "That's not my business. And if you'd just left me alone…"

"I warned you that those men were there! And I told you about the ship, the night before last. I was helping you!"

"I would have seen it for myself!"

"You –"

"Hester?"

They both turned to see Robert at the door of the bakery. He had just turned the sign on the door from 'Closed' to 'Open', and now he was staring at them both. Of course, Hester thought wildly, they were blocking the way into the bakery. They would scare away business. She grabbed Fred by the arm, heedless of the yelp of pain that he let out. "Come on."

"Hester," Robert called. "Hester, wait!" But she was already hurrying away, dragging Fred along with her.

"You're hurting me," Fred gasped out when they got to the bottom of the Cobbler's Lane, and Hester loosened her grip on his arm at last. He stared up at her. "He wanted to help us, your baker! Why didn't you let him?"

"He wanted us to go," Hester corrected. "He's been kind to me, and now I'm returning the favour." She let go of Fred and thrust the objects he had given her back into his hands. "Here."

"What am I supposed to do with these?" he exclaimed.

"Throw them away if you like." Hester tossed over her shoulder as she walked away from Fred. "They're no use to me anymore. And don't go bothering Robert again, whatever you do."

"You're just going to leave me like this?" Fred's voice went up at the end, a little squeaky in disbelief, so that he sounded more like a child than ever, but Hester barely heard him. She had quickened her pace, making straight for Albert Dock.

The sun had already risen, but filtered through the thick white clouds trailing the sky, its light was weak and strained. It was still so dim in the narrow streets below that it might have still been night, and Hester's figure was just one of many, as she slipped along through the growing crowds of merchants, sailors, and dock workers. She felt no fear as she came out by the Mersey, as she drew up close to Davies's warehouse and took her usual route up the stairs that clung to the side of the building. She had never trusted Gentleman Fred, any more than she had trusted any of the other kids in Billy Ross's gang, and so she wouldn't really believe what he had told her, not until she had seen it with her own eyes.

Her ladder was still there. She hoisted herself up and into the loft, and there, in the grey light of morning, she saw her books, an old Dickens, the Bible and *The Pilgrim's Progress,* scattered on the floor and looking as though they had been trampled underfoot, their bindings loose and torn. She saw her white handkerchief soiled by mud. Her devil's dust blanket had been pulled off the pallet and ripped up, so that blue bits of fluff floated in the air around her. And her treasures, everything she had scavenged, save those bits Fred had given her, were all gone.

Hester barely breathed, only looked and looked. She stood frozen to the spot, and time itself seemed to freeze too. And so it was no surprise that she did not hear the creak of the ladder rungs, that she did not feel the presence in the room with her until it had declared itself, by a male voice that was rough and hoarse, as though accustomed to shouting.

"Well!" the voice said. "So they've sent a girl this time! There's more of you dock rats than I thought."

Hester's hand clamped over the pocket of her coat where she had put her knife, and then, slowly, she turned to look at her opponent. She had to crane her neck to look up at him. He was so tall that he was stooping under the low ceiling. He was broader than her, too, and heavier. His face was like old leather, and two small, dark eyes gleamed within those folds of tough skin. In those eyes was the same expression that Hester had seen on the faces of countless other men. But she had never been at close quarters with it before. For six years, since she had left the safety of the workhouse and then fled the cruelty of Mrs. Sharp's, one in quick succession of the other, she had been smart and careful, never staying in one shelter for too long, always guarding herself and her movements, moving fast and keeping herself unnoticed. And then, for the first time in those six years, she had let her guard down, she had stopped listening and watching for a moment, and here she was. He had called her a dock rat, and that was what she was; she was a rat in a trap. Her hand dropped away from her pocket, as she knew that the knife was useless to her. She was shaking so hard that she would not be able to hold it steady.

CHAPTER FOURTEEN

After having had four hours' solid sleep, in between setting the dough and waiting for it to rise, Robert Burrows woke up the next morning to find that, while he was still in love, Miss Simona Fairbank was still the first whose face came to mind when he opened his eyes, he was in a much more reasonable mood than he had been the day before. Things that he had used to care about, in that vast expanse of time before the ringleted, elegant merchant's daughter had walked into his shop, started to come to the fore once more and to claim some, if not all, of his attention. There was his work, which he had sorely neglected the day before and with which he was now determined to get back on track. More distantly, there were his Manchester relations, Cecil, Lesley, and their children. And then there was Hester.

Perhaps some of Robert's new, reasonable state of mind had to do with the fact that he had not been kept in suspense for very long. Within an hour of leaving his bakery yesterday evening, Hester had been back again bearing a new message from his beloved. Not only had Miss Fairbank forgiven him for missing her earlier that evening, but she wanted to meet the following day! No words could have expressed Robert's gratitude towards Hester for bringing him such a wonderful message. And, accordingly, when she asked him if she might stay over that night, he had agreed right away.

Some small part of him knew, of course, that such an arrangement wasn't exactly proper. Hester was no longer the child she had been when he first met her, but a grown woman, and one who would probably soon be looking for a husband. It was hard for Robert to imagine Hester with a husband. In fact, it was hard for him to imagine any part of her life that didn't touch the four walls of his bakery. He had never asked her where she spent her nights, for instance, and she had never seen fit to tell him. He had never asked her if she had any hopes for the future, or if she intended to go on scavenging at Albert Dock until she was bent-backed like old Alice Smith. But though Robert did not know much about Hester's life, he did know that it must have been a cruel one, one that was even, at times, dangerous, and that things would be a little easier for her if she could find someone with whom to share her burdens, a good, honest man to marry.

When Robert had checked the dough, he went into the back room, intending to go up the stairs to his room and get another half-hour's sleep before the bakery opened. Instead, though, he found himself pausing in the threshold and looking at Hester. She had curled up on the settee with her back to him, and as her black hair was obscuring most of her face, he could not see her expression. But as he watched, she turned over, dislodging the blanket that he had put over her. He started back, afraid that she had woken, but after listening to her breathing for a moment, he knew that she was still fast asleep, and as she moved again to rest more comfortably against the cushion on the settee, the dark hair shifted from her face, and he saw that she was smiling. Her lashes were dark against her cheeks, there were tiny creases around her eyelids, and she sighed deeply, contentedly, as though in whatever dream she was dreaming, she had everything she could ever have wanted.

The sound of the shop bell ringing, followed by a "Mr. Burrows!" made Robert start again. He looked up at the clock and saw that almost half an hour had passed. Half an hour! That clock had to be broken. But here was Marcus coming in, just as he always did at this time, so it must really be ten to seven. Robert went to replace the blanket over Hester, and then, clapping his hands together, went out to the shop. It was good that she was getting some rest, he thought as Marcus handed him a tray of scones to put on the window display. God knew she must need it. But he would have to tell her to find somewhere else to stay tonight. It wouldn't be proper to have her here any longer, and what if Miss Fairbank got to hear about it, somehow. What might she think?

Then, hearing a rap on the window, Robert looked up and saw through the glass a boy in a blue frock coat. The boy had a black eye and a nasty weal down one cheek and might have been anywhere from ten to sixteen. He was so skinny and malnourished that it was hard to tell. His hair was pale and brittle like straw. Over the years in Liverpool, Robert had seen many boys like that, but he had never seen any quite as polite as this one, who, when Robert went outside, asked if he might speak to "Miss Grace".

Robert went to wake up Hester. He put a hand on her shoulder, and, as her eyes opened to regard him, that same contented smile remained on her face, but Robert barely noticed. He was thinking about what Cecil had said to him the day before, and how adamant Hester had been in insisting that she was not in any kind of trouble. He was wondering whether her not having had a place to stay last night and this strange, bruised boy showing up on his doorstep the next morning might possibly be connected.

While Hester was outside talking to the boy, Robert brought another tray of pastries to the window display and glanced out at the two of them. The boy was blinking up at Hester and appeared to be rather wary of her. She, for her part, looked furious. Whatever he was telling her, it seemed to make her angrier by the minute, and Robert eventually decided to go out and intervene. He didn't expect that one word from him, "Hester," would make the two of them scatter to the four winds. Baffled, he went out to the street and watched their retreating figures, until the sound of the shop bell, for the second time that morning, recalled him to himself.

In the flow of business that followed, Robert had little time to wonder about Hester and even less to agonise about meeting Miss Fairbank later. But sometime around midday, the bookseller Mr. Moss came in for his usual order of plain scones and lingered at the counter for a moment after Robert had handed him the bag.

"You seem to be in better form today," the old man remarked at last, unsmilingly. He never seemed to smile. Then, indicating the bag, "You remembered."

Robert just nodded, bracing his hands against the counter and looking expectantly at the next customer in the line, but then Mr. Moss took from under his arm a thin, worn volume and held it out to Robert.

"For your friend," he said.

"*The Little Mermaid*, Hans Christian Andersen," Robert read, looking down at the book cover as he took hold of it. "Mr. Moss, who…?" But the bookseller was already shuffling away, and the next customer was pushing up to the counter, so Robert gave the book to Marcus and told him to put it in the back room. There it would remain for the moment, yet another mystery, yet another thing to put out of his mind until he had time to think about it.

CHAPTER FIFTEEN

The big man with the dark, greedy eyes was taking Hester somewhere. He had a grip on her arm so tight that she knew it must already have left a ring of bruises on her skin, but it didn't matter how many times she pleaded with him to loosen his grip, or asked him where they were going, he didn't listen. He marched through the docks, and she stumbled along behind him, and they drew only a few glances from passersby, as such processions were a common occurrence in Liverpool. Hester had seen them many times herself, and she had vowed that she would never let herself be carted away like that. She knew, without a doubt, that she would rather die than be locked up in a House of Correction or worked to the bone in one of those industrial schools that she'd heard whispers about. She looked now at the waters of the Mersey, craning her neck away from the man who was dragging her along.

With one wrench, she might be free. With a running leap, she might be in the water. She couldn't swim. The water was deep, and she would go down quickly.

Her captor, sensing her distraction, tightened his grip on her arm, and Hester felt tears of pain prick her eyes as she forced herself to look ahead again. There was no pulling away from that iron grip. As they approached the turn-off to one of the side-streets that led away from the docks, her mouth went dry. Was he going to bring her straight to the police station on Seel St, to be locked up with Billy Ross and those other boys, just as though she was the same as them? But he turned left instead of right, going towards the Dock Office. A moment later, Hester realised that he was bringing her to Harold Fairbank's warehouse.

If it had been possible for her to feel triumph at that moment, maybe she would have. Maybe she would have tasted some small, bitter measure of it, in realising that she had been right after all. Despite what Robert had said, Hester knew that what she and Fred had seen the other night was a Confederate ship, and so she had thought that whatever mistake or misunderstanding there had been, it must lie elsewhere. Now she knew that Fairbank was using Davies's warehouse, and that the man who currently had an iron grip on her arm must be guarding his cargo. All of this flashed through Hester's head as her captor led her across the busy yard, to the side door through which she had entered once before. They clattered up the dark stairs that led to Mr. Fairbank's offices. On the landing at the top of the stairs, there was no window, but only an oil lamp on a table. In its greasy light, the man turned to look down at her, and he smiled as though at some private joke.

"You're not so bad-looking for a dock rat." With his free hand, he pushed the dark hair off her forehead, and Hester felt her stomach lurch at the touch of his skin on hers. She felt like they were back in the narrow space of her den again, and that the terrible thing she had thought would happen then might still happen. The feeling was only amplified when he added, "We'll have some fun later, you and I."

With that, he tugged her into the office and deposited her in front of the desk, where the unhelpful secretary that she had spoken to once before was writing a letter.

"Found another one," said the man. "She was hanging around Davies's this morning." The secretary nodded.

"Thank you, Farrell. Mr. Fairbank will want to see her himself. I will inform him now." The secretary looked at Hester without a hint of recognition in his eyes. He pointed to a chair in the corner of the room. "Sit down, and don't make any trouble. Farrell, you'd better watch to make sure she doesn't try to get away."

"I won't –" Hester began to say, but her voice was hoarse from lack of use and the words died away. The secretary went into the inner office, opening and closing the door in such a way that Hester only saw a thin bar of room, and only briefly; she saw no people.

The man called Farrell folded his large hands together and stayed by the door. Hester had gone to sit in the chair, and for the next few minutes, she sensed him looking at her and smiling. He never seemed to stop. All the while, she kept her gaze fixed on the door, willing it to open. Her skin began to prickle and itch all over, until she began to feel as though that terrible thing which she feared above all else, what the man had called "fun," was already being done to her, silently, invisibly.

At last the door opened, and the secretary beckoned to her wordlessly. Hester scrambled out of her chair and followed him into the office, feeling Farrell's eyes on her back as she went. It was better lit than the other room, with a large window boasting a view of the dock. Beside the window was a desk, behind which Harold Fairbank sat. Hester had only had a glimpse of him before, but there was not much more to see, really. At close quarters, he looked just as unremarkable as he had from a distance. He had a thick brown moustache, mutton chops, and a portly bearing, the latter of which suggesting that he did not get away from his desk very often, and that when he did it was chiefly to enjoy rich food and wine.

On the other side of Mr. Fairbank's desk a chair had been placed, and in it his daughter sat. She was embroidering a chair cover and did not look up as Hester approached the desk. Mr. Fairbank, on the other hand, looked Hester over with an expression of mild distaste.

"What's your name, girl?"

"Hester Grace, sir."

Out of the corner of her eye, Hester saw Miss Fairbank stop embroidering, and look up. Mr. Fairbank went on, in a tone of resignation rather than outright anger. "And was it you who told Mr. Cecil Locksmith about the ship you saw in port by Davies's warehouse, the night before last?"

Hester hesitated and then answered, "Yes, sir."

Mr. Fairbank exchanged a glance with his daughter and said, in lowered tones which Hester could just about make out, "As I thought." He turned his attention back to Hester. "Tell me, girl, how much has Cecil Locksmith been paying you?"

"How much –?" Hester repeated. Miss Fairbank shifted uncomfortably in her chair. "Mr. Locksmith hasn't been paying me! Why would he…?"

"Come, he must have offered you something, a hot meal, a place to stay, perhaps? Why else would you risk your neck lurking around Albert Dock, spying on me and my workmen?"

"Spying on you, sir?" Hester shook her head very quickly. "No, you don't understand. It's only by chance that I saw that ship the other night. You see I live round these parts."

"It seems that Locksmith chose very well in assigning you to be his eyes and ears." Mr. Fairbank glanced towards his daughter again as he went on, "I believe no one knows

Liverpool's docks as well as these scavengers and petty thieves."

"I'm no thief, sir," Hester said, firmly, and Mr. Fairbank glanced back at her. He leaned back in his chair, his moustache quivering as he sighed.

"There are several members of a gang now under the charge of the constable at Seel Street Station who would say otherwise. One of them, by the name of Ross, has described you and another boy as having stolen a bale of cotton the night before last and brought it to him. This other boy, Small, I think, is the name, was almost apprehended by one of my men last night, but he managed to get away. But you came back, right into the lion's den. Why is that?"

"I live here," Hester said again, desperately.

"I think you wanted to see if there was any more cotton for you to steal. But that wasn't part of yours and Locksmith's deal, was it? Oh, no, I didn't think so. Cecil Locksmith might stoop to spying but he wouldn't stoop to stealing. No, whatever he was giving you, it wasn't enough, was it? You had to have more."

"Papa," Miss Fairbank interjected at last, and he inclined his head in her direction even as he kept his eyes fixed on Hester. "Perhaps there has been some mistake."

"There is no mistake, Simona. This girl," Mr. Fairbank pointed to Hester with a thick, ringed finger, " has been caught red-handed. I'm told she had a hideout in the loft of Davies's warehouse full of stolen wares."

"They weren't stolen, sir."

"She has been seen in company with the boy who got away last night, and I saw her with my own eyes yesterday, from this very window, talking to Locksmith before he came to seek a meeting with me. Now, tell me, how on earth would a girl like this know Cecil Locksmith, unless he sought her out deliberately?"

Hester stared hard at Miss Fairbank, who stared back for only a moment before dropping her eyes. Mr. Fairbank, glancing between them, pointed to Hester again. "You! Weren't you ever taught any manners? Who are you to stare at my daughter like that? You'll look at me, girl, when I'm talking to you."

Hester turned her gaze back on Mr. Fairbank. After a moment's pause, during which there hung such a silence in the room that Hester could hear Miss Fairbank audibly swallowing, Mr. Fairbank went on. "And as if it weren't enough to have this girl sniffing around my business affairs, it seems that Locksmith actually told her to spy on my home, too. For the last two nights, one of my house servants has seen a girl, matching this girl's description, creeping around our garden. Yes, I know, my dear." He turned back to his daughter, who had made an involuntary noise of surprise. "It's most alarming. But you see you were never in any real danger. Our servants were observing the situation carefully, and it was only by my orders that they did not act at once."

"But why – " Miss Fairbank burst out, and then stopped, resuming a moment later in calmer, more wheedling tones, "Why would Cecil Locksmith want to spy on your business, Papa?"

"You're too young to remember this, my dear," said Mr. Fairbank, his eyes still on Hester, as though he thought if he looked away for a moment that she would make a break for it, "but before Byron Davies went bankrupt, Cecil Locksmith was in business with him for a time. Davies had mills and warehouses all over Lancashire back then. Well, now Byron Davies has nothing, because of his own poor investments, investments which, I might add, I warned him against making. And rather than acknowledge his own folly in this, he would rather blame others for his failure. Doubtless he is seeking to discredit me and has brought Locksmith into the fold. That warehouse on Albert Dock is the only thing that remains of his business, and I wouldn't be surprised if he has only rented it out to me for the sole purpose of spying on all our doings."

Miss Fairbank did not contradict her father, just sighed very quietly, and went back to her embroidery. Hester saw that her cheeks had turned crimson.

"You're no fool, are you, girl?" Mr. Fairbank asked Hester, raising his bristly brown eyebrows. "You know enough to know what happens to thieves and vagrants, in any case. They have to be taken off the street, where they will not make trouble anymore. They have to be brought to justice."

"I've told you I'm not a thief."

"Then you're a liar, too, and I don't see why we should waste any more time on you. Weston!" Mr. Fairbank raised his voice as he turned towards the door, and a moment later it opened to admit the secretary again.

"Sir?"

"Tell Farrell to take this girl out of my sight. Bring her to Seel Street, and let them decide what to do with her. I'm sure they'll be –" Mr. Fairbank broke off as a crash sounded from outside on the docks. "What on earth?" He moved to the window. Over his shoulder, Hester could see that below, several crates of coffee had fallen from the back of a cart, and the packers were swarming around to try to right them before the contents spilt. Muttering something under his breath, Mr. Fairbank got to his feet and hurried out of the office, the secretary following on his heels.

"Thank you," said Miss Fairbank to Hester as soon as they were alone. Her cheeks were still red, and she had dropped all pretence of working, her hands limp over the unfinished chair cover. "For not telling him about why you've been coming to Canning Place."

"I gave Robert my word I wouldn't tell anyone about you and him," Hester said stiffly.

"Did you?" Miss Fairbank gazed at her for a moment, before rising from her chair. Her crinoline creaked under swathes of fabric, fabric that quivered like a treetop in a storm as she moved to look out the window. "Well, then you must be a very loyal friend."

There was something about the finality in her tone that frightened Hester more than anything else, and in a flash, she had crossed the room. The merchant's daughter started and stared down at Hester as she dropped to her knees before her.

"Please, miss, please, I can't go with that man. You know I'm innocent. You must say something since I can't."

"Well, I can't say anything either." Miss Fairbank blinked a few times, very rapidly. "I would if I could, but it's impossible. Surely you understand." For a moment, she looked as though she was struggling with some decision, and then she went on, "Just tell Papa that you were working for Cecil Locksmith. I know it's foolish, but he's got this idea in his head now and nothing will budge it. But if you tell him what he wants to hear, maybe he might let you go. Maybe I can persuade him to."

"I can't lie, miss."

"Don't be so foolish. It wouldn't be lying, not really."

The sound of voices and footsteps made Miss Fairbank break off, and she hurried back to her chair, planting herself with another creak and rustle. Hester slowly got to her feet and turned just as Mr. Fairbank came back into the room, followed by the secretary and a grinning Farrell.

"Well, girl," said Fairbank briskly, "so you have nothing to say for yourself?"

Hester felt Miss Fairbank's gaze burning on her, willing her to speak, but she stayed silent. Mr. Fairbank nodded to Farrell, who came forward and seized Hester's arm, right in the same sore spot that he had gripped earlier. She gritted her teeth against the pain but was still silent, silent as they passed Mr. Fairbank and the secretary, silent as they stepped over the threshold.

"Wait!" cried Miss Fairbank, and everyone stopped. She had risen from her chair and was holding out a hand. As her father stared at her, she said, in quavering tones, "You must let her go, Papa. There has been a mistake. And I can explain it all."

CHAPTER SIXTEEN

Robert kept a careful eye on the clock, and at one o'clock sharp he closed up the bakery, but rather than eating his meal in the back room as he usually did, he dispensed with it altogether and took off his apron, grabbing his wool coat from the hook behind the counter. Marcus lived nearby in Ropewalks and always went home to his mother for dinner, so he and Robert walked together as far as Dale Street. Once on his own, Robert walked quickly. He knew he wouldn't have much time. By the time he got to the Botanic Gardens, his hour would almost be up, but even to see Simona even for five minutes would make it all worthwhile. As he walked, Robert glanced into a shop window and took off his cap to pat down his brown hair.

When he got to the Gardens, he walked the perimeter without seeing any sign of Miss Fairbank. Every time he saw a young lady in the distance, his heart would stutter in his chest, but it never turned out to be her. By the time he'd done a full circuit, it had started to rain. Soon the park was clear of people, and Robert turned his steps homeward.

Marcus was pacing up and down outside the door of the bakery when he got back. "I'm not that late, am I?" Robert asked with a wry smile as he took out his keys.

"He came again, Mr. Burrows," his apprentice replied, staring at him. "That boy from this morning."

"Hester's friend?"

"Yes, he was here ten minutes ago, looking for her. I told him to get away."

Robert thought of the boy's bruised face and sighed as he turned the sign on the door. "I suppose that was for the best. He seemed like trouble. But…"

"He'd scare away the customers, sir, hanging around here looking like that."

"Aye, of course you're right, Marcus."

Robert thought repeatedly of the boy, though, as the flow of work resumed. It wasn't just that he didn't like to think of anyone injured like that, wandering forlorn when Robert might be able to help them. This boy knew Hester and might therefore know where to find her, and right now Robert needed to speak to her more than anyone else in the world. This time, he didn't think he would be able to wait until nightfall to know his fate. He needed to know, now, whether there had been some mix-up with Miss Fairbank today, or whether she had simply changed her mind about meeting him.

When the door opened at half-past four to admit Hester, grey with exhaustion, her dark hair half-covering her face, Robert stopped counting change and called Marcus out to man the counter. He strode out, intercepted Hester, and escorted her into the back room, where he sat her down with a cup of tea and the last of the brown bread that he hadn't sold this morning. He waited until some colour had crept back into her face, and then said at last, breathlessly, "Something's happened, hasn't it? I went to the Botanic Gardens today, but she wasn't there."

"She couldn't get away to meet you," Hester said. She took a bite of bread, chewed, and swallowed before continuing. Her eyes, anxious and sympathetic, found Robert's. "I don't think she will be able to get away, for some time."

"Why? What's holding her back? If she doesn't care for me, if this was all nothing after all, you can say it out. I must hear the truth."

"I think she does care for you," Hester said, quietly. "But she told her father a different story."

CHAPTER SEVENTEEN

Hester had been saved, her innocence preserved, and her freedom given back to her, but she couldn't feel grateful towards her saviour, Miss Fairbank, and not just because that saviour held in her soft white hands a gift whose value she couldn't possibly know or recognise, the gift of Robert's love and admiration. It was because Hester's freedom had been won by a lie. Hester hadn't been willing to lie to save her own skin. Was she supposed to feel better because Miss Fairbank had lied in her place?

"I can explain it all, Papa," Miss Fairbank had cried, just as Hester was about to be dragged out of the room. Then she had added, untruthfully, but nobly, or so Hester had thought at the time, "It is all my fault."

Mr. Fairbank, looking bewildered and rather annoyed, had sent Weston and Farrell out of the room. He was on the point of sending out Hester, too, but Miss Fairbank said earnestly, "Please let her stay, Papa. This concerns her, too."

She and her father resumed their places around the desk. Hester stayed standing on the carpet before them, listening intently. Miss Fairbank put aside the chair cover that she had been embroidering and folded her hands in her lap. "You remember Robert Burrows, Papa?" she said. This, in Hester's eyes, was a promising start. "Cecil Locksmith's brother-in-law?"

"The baker?" Mr. Fairbank said pointedly. "Yes."

"When we met the other day, while you and Mr. Locksmith were in your meeting, we got to talking. He, Robert" (*Mr. Burrows*, Hester silently corrected, bristling, "was very pleasant to talk to, and knew quite a lot about books, in fact." (*And why shouldn't he?* thought Hester, resentfully.) "I only meant to be civil, but I'm afraid I must have encouraged him."

"Encouraged him?" Mr. Fairbank repeated, a dangerous edge creeping into his tone.

"Yes. You see, after that he started sending messages to me through this girl, Hester, asking if I could meet with him again. That why the servants saw Hester in the garden. Of course I said no every time, but I don't think he understood."

"That presumptuous, rough-necked *boor* –"

"You mustn't call him such things, Papa," Miss Fairbank said quickly, with a glance towards Hester, who had gone red in her indignation. "Of course Robert would have stopped at once if he had understood how I really felt. The trouble is that I have not been as firm with him as I ought to have been."

Mr. Fairbank opened his mouth as though about to argue, then closed it again. He seemed to consider for a moment before going on, "I have often feared that something like this might happen."

"Yes," said his daughter, almost eagerly, "how many times have you told me that I am too open, too friendly with strangers?"

"Especially with those who are beneath you. That is where you must be most careful, Simona. They might mistake your kindness for something else, as this young Burrows seems to have done."

"Yes," said Miss Fairbank again, "that is exactly what he did. And he meant no discourtesy by it, Papa. I'm sure he would have tried to court me in open if it had been allowed."

"But there is no way it could have been allowed, and so he carried on in secret."

"Yes. And so you see, Papa," she continued, with another anxious glance at Hester, "Hester wasn't to blame at all. She was only doing what Robert asked of her."

Mr. Fairbank glanced towards Hester, too, and ran his knuckles over his moustache. He looked rather deflated.

"Weston," he called after a moment, and his secretary came in, by now looking impatient and utterly bewildered.

"Sir?"

"Tell Farrell he can go."

"But sir, the girl –"

"I'm sure he has other business to attend to, does he not? And at any rate, that shouldn't concern you, Weston. Just do as I say." When the door had swung closed again, Mr. Fairbank turned to his daughter without looking directly at her. "Simona, if you would be so good as to show this girl out..."

"Thank you, Papa!"

"... and then come back here so that we may talk about all this. Properly." Mr. Fairbank swept one more disdainful glance at Hester and then took out some papers from his desk, evidently intent to bury himself in some unnecessary tasks, until she was out of his sight.

"So he let you go after that?" Robert asked later when Hester told him the story. She had left out some bits, letting Robert believe that Mr. Fairbank had summoned her to his office in a much more civilised way. Hester wasn't quite sure why she had done that. Maybe it was because of the light that had entered Robert's eyes as soon as she said that she still thought Miss Fairbank cared for him. Maybe it was because she could not yet put into words the chill that had swept over her when she had beheld her den destroyed, or the itchy, prickly feeling that the man, Farrell, had given her. Either way, Hester told herself, it was not lying, not really. She was not lying in the same way that Miss Fairbank had lied.

"Aye, he let me go," she told Robert. "He didn't say sorry, just told me to stay out of trouble."

"Fancy him thinking Cecil was the type to spy on his business," Robert marvelled. "And to get you to do it, too! It's a good thing it was cleared up." He did not smile, but his eyes, by now, were positively beaming, as he added, "And it was brave of Si – I mean, Miss Fairbank – to tell her father the truth." In an instant, his eyes had darkened again, like sunlight dimmed by a cloud, as he looked back at Hester. "If she hadn't, then you might have been sent away. And it would have been my fault, for sneaking around instead of keeping things in the open."

Hester struggled for a moment to follow his logic. "Then, you mean to go on courting Miss Fairbank?"

"I mean to try. You said you think she still cares for me, didn't you? If you believe that, then I believe you." Robert smiled at Hester, one of his old smiles that was just for her. "Of course she had to say those things to her father to protect her own modesty. I'll have to see her father as soon as I can, to show him that I am serious, but I don't see why not. There isn't such a huge gap between a baker and a merchant's daughter. And, if there is, well," Robert looked around at the back room, and glanced towards the door to the bakery, through which Marcus could be heard talking to the customers. "Well, then maybe it's time I thought about closing up this place."

Hester, feeling as one feels when all the air has been knocked out of their lungs by a cruel blow, took a moment to find her voice. "Closing the bakery?"

Robert looked back at her quickly. "Well, that is, I'm just thinking about the possibilities. If Simona – if Miss Fairbank and her father would prefer me to have a more respectable profession, well, Marcus might take over things here. He's almost old enough. And of course nothing else would have to change. You and I could still be friends!"

A silence hung between them, during which Hester thought of several bitter, sarcastic things to say to that. *Not such a huge gap between a baker and a merchant's daughter, maybe, but what about a baker and a scavenger from Albert Dock?* In the end, though, she just said, briskly, "So you'll go to see Mr. Fairbank tomorrow?"

"Aye, I'll go during my dinner hour, but if he won't see me then, I'll wait for as long as it takes. I'll leave Marcus to run things here and maybe..." Robert paused, as though a thought had just occurred to him. "Could you help him, for an hour or two?"

"Of course," said Hester, just as she always did and always would do whenever he asked her something. As a reward she got another smile and a squeeze of her hand. Then Robert, as he got to his feet, added,

"And of course, you should stay here for the moment, until that boy is caught. He came looking for you again today, you know."

"You mean Fred Small?" said Hester, staring at Robert.

"Aye, the boy who came for you this morning. That's why you stayed here last night, isn't it? You were trying to avoid him?"

"I..."

"You don't have to tell me any more if you don't want to," Robert said hastily. "I know you'd never get involved with those gangs. But maybe you'd best stay away from Albert Dock until it's all blown over."

He smiled over his shoulder at her and passed out into the bakery before Hester could say anything else. Left alone, she raised her hand, which was still tingling from his touch, and put it to her cheek.

CHAPTER EIGHTEEN

L ater that night, after Robert had gone upstairs to get a few hours' sleep, Hester was lying awake on the settee when she heard a rap on the window of the back room. Though bone-tired from the day's events, she hadn't been able to settle her mind to rest, and now she scrambled up, groping around for a match and a wick. Once the oil lamp was lit and the darkness of the room illuminated, Hester went to the door and put her hand on the latch. "Who is it?" she hissed out through the keyhole.

"Mr. Small," came the response, and Hester sighed before opening up the door.

"What are you doing here? I told you to stay away." As Fred stepped into the circle light, she blinked in surprise. His face was still bruised, but the nasty swelling around the bruises had gone down, and the cuts were no longer as angry or red. His hair looked neater, too, and he had acquired a hat from somewhere. "You got yourself cleaned up!"

"I have found that one can almost always rely on the kindness of strangers," he said, and then pressed a sixpence into her palm. "I came merely to give you this."

"What?" Hester started to say. He was already turning to leave.

"It was given to me by Harry Cronshaw," Fred said over his shoulder, "in exchange for those things left over from your invention, which I brought to him after you thrust them back into my care."

Hester stared down at the sixpence and bit her lip. Then she hurried out the door, following Fred for a few paces. "Here. You should have it. You need it more than I do."

"Keep it," he said, glancing back at her with a shrug of his skinny shoulders. "I am to blame in this affair, after all." He looked back towards the pool of light just within the door. "And I can assure you, I won't disturb you or your baker anymore." With a tip of his hat, Fred Small was gone, leaving Hester alone in the yard.

CHAPTER NINETEEN

For the next week, Robert Burrows went to Harold Fairbank's offices every afternoon to try and get a meeting with him. Every single time, the secretary would tell him that Mr. Fairbank was busy, and Robert would wait all the same, as one hour turned into two and then into three. At some point, the secretary would always make him leave, but after that, Robert would just go outside and wait there instead, getting in the way of all the dockers as he gazed at the upper windows of the warehouse. He grew very familiar with Albert Dock, with the ceaseless screaming of the gulls, the smell of brine, the creaking of the cranes and the shouts of sailors. He started to wonder how anyone, least of all Hester, who was so quiet, could manage to make their home in such a place, which changed from day to day, and which did not sleep at night. Robert would only go home when the lights of Mr. Fairbank's warehouse went out, but on his walk back through the dock he would wade through a crowd of thousands, different languages reaching his ears every few steps.

During that time, he did not see Simona Fairbank at all, but neither did he despair. Gone was the horrible suspense of those first few days after he had met her. No longer did he vacillate between pleasure and pain in contemplation of the next step in their courtship. Robert liked to think that this was because everything was aboveboard now. His actions before had been those of a lovesick boy, sending his friend to carry messages between him and his beloved, but seeking out the beloved's father in order to ask for her hand was what a man ought to do. Because Robert, who, only a week ago, had seen marriage as a grim eventuality, now saw it in the immediate, as encompassing his whole future. Mr. Fairbank might be ignoring him now, but Robert knew that he would prevail. He would do whatever was needed to make himself worthy of Simona, and this new certainty, where before there had only been suspense, made him sleep better at night.

There was also the fact that, during those hours when Robert was keeping his vigil in Albert Dock, he knew that the bakery was in good hands. Marcus had stepped up to the mark, certainly, but it was Hester's contribution that proved the most surprising to Robert. She was canny. She could see that a thing needed to be done without being told, and she was quick about counting notes and giving out change. As well as that, the customers liked her. She seemed to have something to say to everybody. One afternoon, before heading for Albert Dock, Robert stood outside one of the windows of the bakery, unobserved, to watch Hester work, and he could find nothing to criticise in her.

On the third morning of this new routine, Robert gave Hester a new dress that he had bought the day before, and she acted like he had gifted her the moon. It was just a plain brown calico, but she shook it out and held it up to herself and said she had seen something like it in the dressmaker's where she used to work.

"Dressmaker's?" Robert repeated. "You never told me about that. When did you work there?"

Hester's startled brown eyes met his, as though she had revealed more than she meant to, and she murmured something about its having been after she had left the workhouse. Robert knew better than to press the issue, and instead he handed her over the pair of flat shoes and the shawl that he had found in the trunk upstairs. "My sister Lesley left them here on one of her visits. They're clean, but let me know if the shoes don't fit and I can buy you another pair. You should have good shoes when you're on your feet all day."

"Why are you doing this?" Hester asked him as she looked down at the items in her hands, and there was something in the tone of her voice that made Robert feel strange and unsteady for a moment. Quickly, he laughed it off.

"You've helped me a lot. Aren't I allowed to do something for you? Anyway, it's not as unselfish as you think. You're behind the counter, and you're the first thing people will see when they come into this shop. It's important to look... well, you understand?"

"Yes," said Hester, in an entirely different voice, one that sounded like all its emotion had been flattened out. She turned away and said she would go and get changed. But Robert noticed, over the next few days, that as soon as six o'clock rolled around and the bakery closed, at which time he would usually be back from Albert Dock, Hester would change back into her own clothes, the grey shirt and man's waistcoat and trousers that she had always worn.

When he was coming back one day, later than usual, for he had tracked Mr. Fairbank to his solicitor's office near Sefton Park, only to be met there by another unhelpful secretary, Robert came back down Cobbler's Lane via Dale Street and, consequently, passed Mr. Moss's bookstand. The bookseller was carrying a crate inside, but he paused in his activity to call out "Good evening" to Robert. A little flummoxed by this friendliness, Robert returned the greeting nonetheless, and then Mr. Moss asked,

"How did your friend like the book?"

"What book?" Robert said, and the old man's dark brows drew down around his eyes until his face had resumed its customary expression of displeasure.

"The one I gave you last week, free of charge, I might add. The one about the mermaid."

"The mermaid? Oh, I remember now," Robert said apologetically. "I'll make sure she gets it as soon as possible."

"You do that."

Robert, who had begun to walk away, paused again and half-turned. "It is Hester you mean, isn't it? Just to make sure."

"Yes," said Mr. Moss gruffly, "Who else?"

"Thank you." Robert hesitated for a moment more. "I can pay you for that book, if you like." But Mr. Moss's brows drew down even further at this suggestion, and he shook his head before picking up the crate of books again.

The bakery was closed up when Robert got back, and it appeared to be empty, but by the sounds coming from the back yard he knew that Hester and Marcus were not too far away. He passed through the bakery and came out, swinging his key in his hand, to find them kicking around a ball with some of the neighbourhood children. The yard was not really big enough, and so they all kept running into each other as they played, with each collision provoking great hilarity. Marcus was the first to spot

Robert, and he hastily detached himself from the group as soon as he had done so, untying his apron and slinging it over his arm. "Sorry, Mr. Burrows," he said as he hurried for the back door, but Robert stopped him as he was passing and asked,

"What did you do with that book? The one that I told you to put in the back room last week?"

Marcus was a bit red already, evidently embarrassed at having been caught out in a children's game, but now he went redder still and said "Sorry" again.

"What are you saying sorry for?" Robert asked, more sharply than he had intended, for now, on the sixth day of his vigil, his nerves were starting to wear thin.

"I put it in my coat pocket for safekeeping," Marcus said, without meeting Robert's gaze, "and then I forgot about it and took it home with me. I kept meaning to bring it back every morning and then forgetting. And then, last Sunday, when we were supposed to be reading our Bible, I got bored and started reading that book instead. I know it's a girl's book, but once I started, I couldn't stop. And after I read it, my sister wanted to read it, too. She thought the ending was sad, but I liked it."

"Do you still have the book at home?" Robert felt that they had wandered from the point somewhat.

"Yes, sir."

"Well, bring it in tomorrow and mind you don't forget again. It's meant for Hester."

A sudden commotion made them both look around, to see that several of the neighbourhood boys had tackled Hester to the ground. At least, they appeared to have tackled Hester to the ground. There were so many of them over her that she wasn't visible at all. Robert rushed forward without a moment's thought. "Hey! Let her go!"

The children turned startled faces towards him and, after he had repeated himself once or twice more, obeyed. But Hester, when Robert pulled her to her feet, was laughing. She was still clutching the ball to her chest. Her hair, which she had tied back, was starting to come loose around her face.

"Are you all right?" he asked her, rather unnecessarily, as in fact he didn't think she had ever looked better, happier, his mind corrected a moment later, alarmed by its own turn of phrase.

Hester nodded as she let the ball fall from her hands and kicked it across to the boys, but before they could kick it back, Robert took her by the elbow and steered her towards the door. "Come and have something to eat. Marcus, I reckon it's time for you to be heading home."

"See you again tomorrow," Hester shouted to the boys as she followed him in, and Marcus echoed her call.

"Why don't you wear the clothes I got you?" Robert asked Hester once they were alone, with yesterday's meat pie on the table between them. She paused at the question and looked up at him, her fork halfway to her mouth. Since it was a mild evening, Robert had left the door ajar, and it faced onto an empty yard. The boys had taken their ball across the street, but the occasional whoop or gale of laughter still drifted over, and Robert had to admit it was quite a friendly sound.

"I do wear them," Hester said, confusedly.

"I don't just mean when you're working. I mean, I didn't just get them for you for that reason."

She scraped her fork on her plate and they both winced at the sound. "But I thought you said, before…"

"Don't pay too much attention to the things I say," Robert said, and he saw a smile flash across her face then. It was gone in the next instant, but it melted something between them, a chill that had crept up over the last few days. He leaned forward now, and their arms grazed. He had his sleeves rolled up and so did she, so, for a moment, his bare skin was on hers. Her head flew up, and Robert hastily withdrew his arm.

"Hester," he said, "I know you must think I take you for granted." She made a noise of protest, and he went on, "But you've been wonderful this past week, really you have. I want you to know that this won't go on for much longer."

"Then Mr. Fairbank has finally agreed to see you?" she asked, after the briefest of pauses.

"No." Robert sighed. "But I can't keep running into a brick wall. And, what, for someone I've only met once?"

He heard Hester's intake of breath but found he was too embarrassed to look at her. "Well, it's true, isn't it? And it might be true, too, that she is pretty, elegant, and kind and all the rest, and that I think of her often, and that I'd like to get the chance to meet her again. But I'm starting to wonder if maybe I've put the cart before the horse. I've never really had romances, you see, the way other lads do. There was a girl, when I was growing up in Vauxhall, but she got sick and died and I suppose since then I haven't –" Robert knew he was babbling now. He pushed aside his plate, since he had no more appetite, and got to his feet, walking as far as the open door. He halted when he could feel the cool evening air on his face. "What I'm trying to say is that I don't know how to tell what's real from what isn't."

Hester's voice, when it came from behind him, sounded slightly strangled. "I know you don't mean that."

"I do." Robert ran a hand over his face. "What if this is all just some silly..."

"It's not." He heard the scrape of chair legs against the floor as she got up. "It's real. And you've done so much! You can't give up now."

Robert shook his head, wordlessly, as he stared out at the yard. Hester's footsteps sounded behind him as she drew a bit closer. "He won't see you?" she said, and there was something fierce in her voice now. "Mr. Fairbank? Then you write him a letter. Explain how you feel, state your intentions towards his daughter. And if he still doesn't accept you after that, then the more fool him. He should be proud to have someone like you in his family."

Robert turned around and gazed at Hester. She was standing only a few paces away from him now, and she met his gaze steadily. "You're kind," he said after a moment. "Very kind, to say that, but you know that not everyone would agree with you."

"I don't care," she said firmly. "They're fools, they're all fools, if they don't see what I see."

Robert couldn't help what he did next. He stepped forward and drew her into his arms, held her right to his heart. It was only for a few seconds, but he knew right away that he had gone too far because she didn't move at all. When he released her a moment later, she stood stiff as a board, looking as though a gust of wind might have snapped her in half. "I'm sorry," Robert said, and Hester's eyes met his, very briefly. "I shouldn't have."

"Don't be sorry," she told him, even as she turned away and made for the door. Robert followed her out into the bakery.

"Wait! Where are you going? I didn't mean to frighten you."

"You didn't frighten me," she said without turning.

"Well, then, what's the matter?" He caught up with her at the door, which he had left unlocked earlier for Marcus going home. Robert took hold of Hester's arm before she could open the door. She turned but did not look up at him. "Hester, we're friends, aren't we?"

"Yes," she said. "We're friends." Her voice cracked on the last word as though on a sob. Robert stared. Hester never cried. He was so shocked that he let her go, and by the time he got his wits about him again, she had disappeared into the darkening street.

CHAPTER TWENTY

S he'd thought that she knew the meaning of pain, but here was agony such as she had never felt before. Hester bent double with the force of it as soon as she left the bakery. Hot tears filled her eyes but did not drop down her cheeks. She half-sobbed, half-coughed as she staggered along. This past week had been a gift. Sharing Robert's days, being closer to him than she had ever been, even though she had lost everything else–her home, her inventions–had brought her happiness undreamed of. And, just now, he had done something impossible. He had actually taken her in his arms. How could such a thing have happened, and why had it only made everything worse? Was she really so greedy as to always want more, more, no matter how much he gave her? Would it never be enough, until he was kneeling before her?

Shocked into a stop by that last thought, Hester slowly straightened, still holding her stomach. That was the one thing she knew could never happen. Robert would never kneel before her to ask for her hand. She had not even let herself imagine him doing something like that for a long time, so why was the picture in her mind now? Because he had just held her for the first time, Hester reminded herself, and as she started to walk again, another wave of agony struck her, so intense that she groaned aloud.

She stopped at the door of the draper's shop and knocked for a few minutes before it opened to Mrs. Kelly. Hester knew the woman. She was a regular at the bakery, but she looked Hester up and down now as though she didn't know her. Judging by the smell of cooking food and the look of displeasure on her face, she had evidently been interrupted in her dinner, and when Hester asked for Mr. Moss, Mrs. Kelly shouted down the cellar stairs to her neighbour, "Another one for you!" before beating a retreat up the stairs to her own lodgings.

Mr. Moss came creaking up the stairs, carrying a candle even though it wasn't fully dark yet. He peered at Hester as he came out onto the shop floor. "It's late. What do you want?"

"Can I stay here?" said Hester breathlessly, and he looked positively bewildered. "Just for tonight?"

"Why would you want to stay here?"

"I can pay." She fished in the pocket of her waistcoat, but all she found was a sixpence, the sixpence Fred Small had given her last week. Hester took it out and stared at it.

"I don't want your money, girl," said Mr. Moss. "But where's that coat I gave you?"

"Oh, I forgot. I must have left it." Hester gestured behind her, vaguely, and the bookseller tutted.

"You're as careless as that baker of yours."

"He's not my baker," Hester exclaimed, and, before she could help it, burst into fresh tears. Mr. Moss's look of bewilderment became one of outright discomfiture, and he glanced around before gesturing to Hester to follow him.

"All right, all right, stop that and come on. I don't want Patricia Kelly coming down and complaining again."

"What did she mean when she said, 'another one'?" Hester asked him, tearily, as she followed him down the stairs to the cellar.

"Oh, a boy showed up on my doorstep last week, all beaten up and black-eyed but ever so polite. A very strange boy he was. He said he'd got separated from his friends. I reckon he was in some kind of trouble, but I don't ask questions, me. He stayed here just one night and left for Manchester the next morning."

"Manchester?" Hester repeated, staring at the bookseller's bent back.

"Aye, that's what he said."

They passed through a narrow hall and into Mr. Moss's lodgings, which comprised one room. Hester could see now why he needed a candle as it was very dark down here. There were a couple of windows, high up, whose upper halves looked out onto the street. Through the dim, she saw crates and crates of books, and so many candle stubs, propped on every available space, in candlesticks and on cracked plates, that she thought it was a wonder the place hadn't caught alight. Then again, with the smell of damp that hung over everything, maybe it wasn't such a wonder after all.

In one corner was an iron bedstead, and between it and the stove was a sagging armchair, over which Mr. Moss now draped a blanket before bustling over to the stove. "You'll be warm enough here, I reckon. Do you want something to eat?"

"No, thanks," said Hester, whose insides still felt like they were on fire. She hadn't even finished her food back at Robert's, though a broken heart had never stopped her from eating before. Maybe, she thought with a wrench, that was because she was only learning now what a truly broken heart felt like. What had the last few years of pining for Robert been about, then?

"I won't ask what happened with the baker," said Mr. Moss, with his back to her as he closed the door of the stove. "Like I said, I don't ask questions."

Hester sank into the armchair gratefully and pulled the blanket over her, staring at the red glow of the stove. A few minutes of blessed silence ensued, before Mr. Moss carried on, now from the other side of the room. By the clatter of crockery it sounded like he was cleaning the dishes. "But you know, girl, you're going to have to face it sooner or later."

"Not if I go away," Hester said, leaning her head against the armchair, and as soon as she had spoken the words, she knew them to be true. Going away was the only thing she could do now. Going away, like Fred had already done. He had probably been sitting in this exact same spot last week, unsure of his future, but when he had come to her at the bakery that night, she had given him no help. She had chased him off. "Maybe I'll go to Manchester, too."

Mr. Moss just snorted. "Manchester? Why would you go there? There are no jobs. More mills are closing every day because of this American war. You're best off staying here."

Hester, who was too tired to argue, just sighed. "Did your baker give you that book?" Mr. Moss asked a while later when she was nearly asleep.

"He's not my baker," Hester said again, through a yawn. She had settled back against the armchair, and the other part of Mr. Moss's sentence had slipped past her notice.

CHAPTER TWENTY-ONE

R obert left the back door unlocked in case Hester wanted to come back. He had no idea where she might have gone to, but he reasoned that she would probably return the next morning at the latest. There was nothing else he could do. He had acted without thinking in embracing her like that, and though she had insisted that she was not frightened, Robert could see no other explanation for her behaviour. He would just have to apologise again the next time he saw her. He knew very little of Hester's past, but he could hazard a few guesses as to how she might have been treated back then, and why a man suddenly embracing her now might cause her some alarm. The thought made him quiet and sombre all night, for after he had set the dough, he sat up for much of it, composing his letter to Mr. Fairbank. He scrapped what he had written and started again more times than he could count, his pen scratching along the page as the candle flame flickered a few inches away, its small circle of light pressing back the dark night.

The sound of the shop bell made Robert jerk awake to find that it was daylight. He had slumped over the table and fallen asleep, and though he did not remember blowing out his candle, evidently he had had the presence of mind to do so. He rubbed his palm over one eye and then the other. "Hester?" he called, but the door to the back room flew open to admit Marcus instead.

"I didn't forget!" his apprentice called out triumphantly by way of a greeting, and then his eyes alighted on Robert and his expression changed. "Mr. Burrows, are you all right? Have you been sitting up all night? What are you writing?"

Against this onslaught of questions, Robert had no defence but to gather the various scraps of paper to his chest so that the writing on them was covered. "Nothing, nothing," he said blearily. "Will you check on the dough? It might have burnt by now. I don't know how long I've been asleep."

Marcus shrugged off his coat and put down his bag before scrambling to obey Robert's orders. From the kitchen, his voice carried as he heaved open the door to the oven. "I didn't forget the book, Mr. Burrows!"

"The book?" Robert repeated, uncomprehending. He had gotten to his feet and was leafing through the various letters he had started and then scrapped last night, trying to see there was a single one among them that was even halfway acceptable.

"The book, the one you told me to bring back today!" called his apprentice.

"Oh. Well, then, where is it?"

Marcus came to the doorway of the kitchen, carrying a tray of white loaves that looked browner than Robert would have liked but, at least, were not burnt. "I gave it to Hester on my way."

Robert gave a start. "You've seen Hester?"

"Aye, just now. She was going towards Dale Street, and she looked in a hurry. I thought you must have sent her on some errand."

"I didn't," Robert murmured. He was still holding one of the letters. Now he pocketed it and, in a swift movement, gathered up the rest of the scraps and threw them into the embers of the fireplace. Then he slipped out the back door and hurried up Cobbler's Lane. He thought he would be sure to catch her on Dale Street. She couldn't have gone that far in a few minutes, but when he emerged onto the thoroughfare and looked right and left, he could not spot her dark head among the bobbing top hats and bonnets of passersby. At the sound of a whip lash, Robert stepped aside to avoid being splashed by an oncoming carriage. He ran a hand over his hair and then turned back.

In the bakery, Marcus was waiting behind the counter with a worried frown. "What's wrong, Mr. Burrows?"

"I don't know," said Robert, honestly, as he passed through to the back room and then halted, looking for a moment at the calico dress, shawl, and shoes, all in a neat little pile at the end of the settee. Then, patting the square in his pocket, he called to Marcus, "Can you deliver a letter for me?"

CHAPTER TWENTY-TWO

Hester woke up a few times throughout the night, and each time she found herself in thick, deep darkness. The light of the stove had gone out, and only the smell of damp and the faint sound of Mr. Moss's snoring reminded her of where she was, but when she settled back to sleep, that same darkness followed her, pressing down on her eyes, her chest, and her stomach. She dreamt that she got up in it and hurried out, up the creaky steps down which Mr. Moss had led her and into the deserted street. There was a light on in Robert's bakery, and she ran straight there, and he was waiting for her at the back door.

"It was so dark there," she told him, and he pulled her in and pressed her to his heart again, just as he had done before.

"I know," he said, dropping a kiss on her head, and Hester buried her face in his shoulder. When she woke once more, she lay in the darkness for a few minutes, convinced that her dream had really happened. It had to have happened. It had felt so real.

As daylight began to filter in through the high windows of Mr. Moss's lodgings, Hester got up and searched around for a minute or two. She found paper and pen on a cluttered shelf, and wrote out a brief note of thanks to Mr. Moss, who still lay asleep. Then she tiptoed up the stairs and out of the draper's shop.

Her dream had been only a dream, after all, but now she was retracing the steps that she had taken in it. She went to the bakery and walked around to the back door. Slowly, soundlessly, she opened it to see that Robert was sleeping at the table with his head on his arms, a piece of paper stuck to his cheek and more paper strewn around his hands. At the other end of the table was a candle which he must have forgotten to blow out, and it was nearly burned to a stub now.

It was just her coat that Hester had come back to get, but as she moved to blow out the candle, she paused for a minute to look at Robert's face. A faint frown creased his forehead. He was dreaming about something that worried him. Hester straightened up, her coat over her arm. With her free hand, she touched his shoulder very lightly as she was passing by, and she wished fervently that whatever dreams he might dream in the future, they would be happy ones.

Her mind was full of vague, unformed plans. She knew she would not visit Robert's bakery anymore, and she would rather die than go back to the workhouse. That much was still true, but she couldn't tell what else she was fit for. She could go on scavenging just as she'd always done, making something from nothing, but she would need a new place to sleep. Billy Ross and his gang might be locked up in Seel Street, but there were other gangs like his dotted up and down the docks. Hester knew where to find them if she had to. They might give her somewhere to stay and something to eat, though of course there would be a price to pay in return. She would have to join them; she would no longer really be free.

Last night she had thought that she might go to Manchester and seek out Fred Small. She saw this now for the mad plan that it was, but as she was coming up Cobbler's Lane, she met Marcus on his way to work.

"Good morning, Hester!" he called out cheerfully.

"Good morning," she murmured, about to pass on.

"Wait. I have something for you."

Hester turned back around, confused, and saw that Marcus was rummaging around in his satchel. He drew out a book, a precious book that Hester had spent years trying to find, and he passed it into her hands.

"Mr. Burrows said to give this to you," he said, with an innocent smile, before continuing on his way.

Hester hadn't realised until that moment that inside her had remained a small scrap of hope, that by staying in Liverpool, she could still choose to be close to Robert and watch him from afar, even if she couldn't bear to be any more than that. But that scrap had fluttered away into the wind now that she was holding in her hands the book about the mermaid. Robert had read it. He must have. His giving it to her now must be a kind of apology, an acknowledgement that, like the prince in the story, he would never see her as anything other than his dear little friend. Hester decided, in that moment, that she would go to Manchester.

CHAPTER TWENTY-THREE

G iven the fact that he had been ignored in all of his attempts to see Mr. Fairbank in person, Robert wasn't really expecting that a letter to that same gentleman should meet with a kinder reception. He had written it more out of a need to assure himself that he had tried everything, and so, after he had had Marcus deliver it to Canning Place that morning, Robert did his best to put the matter out of his mind.

He was naturally surprised and a little alarmed when, in the time creeping up to his dinner hour, the door of the bakery opened to admit Miss Simona Fairbank.

This was only Robert's second time meeting her, which was a strange thought, and there could not have been a greater contrast between the first moments of those two meetings. Then, the young lady's eyes had danced with good humour, but now they blazed with anger. Then, she had stood by the door, quiet and demure, while her father did the talking; now, she swept past the other customers and right up to the counter with the air of an offended duchess, as she freezingly told "Mr. Burrows" that she must speak to him at that moment.

Robert left Marcus to man the counter and showed Miss Fairbank into the back room. As she stepped in, moving sideways so that her crinoline would not catch in the doorway, her eyes scanned the place, and Robert was instantly glad that he had cleared away Hester's good clothes. The sight of them might have given rise to uncomfortable questions.

"What was the meaning of this?" Miss Fairbank demanded, before he'd even had time to close the door. He hastened to do so now, and when he turned back it was to see that she was holding up an envelope with a partly folded letter inside.

"That was intended for your father," Robert said quietly.

"I'm aware, Mr. Burrows, and all I can say is that it is fortunate it fell into my hands first rather than his. He is very angry with you."

"Angry with me?"

"You sound surprised, Mr. Burrows, but I'm sure I can't understand why. Did you expect that we wouldn't hear of your little arrangement here? Did you think that waiting outside my father's office, day in, day out, would be sufficient proof of your constancy, and that no other should be required?"

"Please sit down, Miss Fairbank," Robert said placatingly, "and then we can discuss this properly. There seems to have been a misunderstanding somewhere."

"There is no misunderstanding this time, Mr. Burrows, and I will not sit down, thank you. I do not intend to stay long. I have only come to beg you to leave myself and my father in peace. I should not like to see Papa driven to violence, but if you continue to plague us, I am afraid that he might take matters into his own hands."

"I've done nothing wrong," said Robert quietly, after a painful silence. "Reached too high, maybe, in thinking of you, but I couldn't help that."

"I will hear none of your excuses now, Mr. Burrows. They are words, nothing more." Miss Fairbank's voice had risen in her distress. "You say you were thinking of me, and all the while, in your own home you have been entertaining another. But I cannot even say it; it is too shocking."

Her meaning was starting to dawn on Robert now. "Is this about Hester staying here?"

Miss Fairbank took a few steps towards the door and then stood with her back to him. "Then you admit it."

"No. No." Robert started forward as though to touch her arm, then thought better of it. "Please, Miss Fairbank, just listen to me for a moment. I admit it was an improper arrangement. But Hester had nowhere else to go, and I thought only of what was due to her."

"What was due to her? What about what was due to me?" Miss Fairbank had taken out a handkerchief. Robert saw the flash of white as she raised it to dab her eyes.

"Well," he said, as gently as he could, "I'm sure that such a thing never entered my head when I agreed to let Hester stay here, Miss Fairbank. Firstly, I didn't imagine you would get to hear about it."

"Then you were foolish. Everyone has heard about it. My servants have been laughing at me. My maid is friends with your neighbour, the draper, Mrs. Kelly, and Mrs. Kelly told her that when she was buying her bread here one morning, she got a glimpse into your back room. She said that it was obvious someone had been sleeping there." Miss Fairbank half-turned again, sweeping another glance around the room.

"And so she was," Robert said. "Hester, I mean. But I promise you, there was nothing. Hester and I are friends, nothing more. And, in any case, I'm not the kind of man who would take advantage of such an arrangement."

"I know you are not. And I own I was surprised. I did not want to believe such a report of you." Miss Fairbank finally turned to face him, unshed tears gleaming in her eyes. "My father has been very angry. You cannot imagine how angry he has been. He heard about it before even I did, from one of the servants, too."

"Is that why he has been refusing to see me?" Robert exclaimed. "I hope you will explain things to him. I hate to think of anyone believing I could do something like that, least of all someone I think of highly of as your father."

"I will explain things to him," said Miss Fairbank measuredly, "as long as you promise not to entertain such an arrangement again."

"Of course. I'll tell Hester as soon as I see her that she must find somewhere else to stay, but, though, you know, if she can't, I can't very well turn her away."

Miss Fairbank just looked at him for a long moment. "I don't want to see her here again," she said at last.

"You don't expect me to be so unfeeling towards a friend."

"I do expect it, when that friend is in love with you!"

Robert almost laughed, though there could not have been a worse moment to do so. "In love with me? But you don't understand. I've known Hester for years!"

"Is that supposed be my security?" Miss Fairbank asked incredulously. "Your long acquaintance, much longer than our own?"

"No, I just mean, you must be mistaken." Robert held her gaze, steadily. "Really."

"There is no mistake," she said, looking back at him just as steadily.

Robert sighed and finally dropped his eyes from hers, taking a few steps back as he ran a hand through his hair. "I can promise you that Hester won't stay here another night. I'll find some other arrangement, but I can't promise you that you won't see her again. She's my friend and she's been coming around here for a long time. I can't just..." He flapped a hand uselessly but couldn't seem to find the right words.

"If that is your answer," said Miss Fairbank, in that same freezing tone in which she had first addressed him, "then I'm obliged to you, sir, for making everything so clear to me. Good day."

CHAPTER TWENTY-FOUR

Hester Grace paid for her train fare to Manchester by selling her hair. She got it shorn short, almost to her scalp, and, together with her men's clothes and the cap that she had found abandoned on the pavement on South Street, the desired effect was produced. She looked like a boy, and nobody bothered her on the journey from Liverpool. She had never been on a train before. She sat in the open third-class carriage as the winter wind whistled overhead and watched the countryside flash past. October had turned to November in a flash, it seemed, since this whole business with Robert and the Fairbank and Cecil Locksmith had started. Looking at the bare trees and fallow fields that passed by, Hester thought, as she had not thought for a long time, of her parents and who they might have been. She wondered if they had ever taken this journey.

Night had fallen by the time they approached Manchester, for Hester had gotten a pretty late train. It was only thanks to the conductor's announcement that she knew they had reached their destination. A fog had come down over everything, and apart from a patch of dark, angry red in the night sky, there was no indication that anything lay ahead at all. She might have been in the middle of nowhere, rather than the second city of England, or at least she thought so until she got out onto the crowded platform.

She was used to seeing crowds in Albert Dock, but that was in the open air, and this was in a narrow space, between trains whose engines purred and hissed out their discontent in noxious fumes. Hester was jostled as she got out of the carriage, and she nearly fell flat on her face. The platform was swarming with people, and the blare of noise, after the relative quiet of the train, made her feel a bit light-headed. She followed the stream of people out of the station, and as that stream turned to a trickle, she took her own way. She walked down a narrow lane which seemed to promise an alehouse or two, if nothing else, where she might have something to drink or eat to warm her stomach, but she found only buildings with dark windows, and when she passed from the lane onto a broader thoroughfare, she just saw more of the same. Craning her neck to look up at them, Hester wondered what they could be. Offices? Warehouses? Counting houses?

Somewhere in this city, she reasoned to herself, there had to be light and life and noise. She would walk until she had found it.

CHAPTER TWENTY-FIVE

As the weeks passed with no sign of Hester, Robert's feelings ran the gamut from concern to sorrow to anger. On this latter they finally settled, towards the end of November. By then, he no longer expected to see or hear from her. Evidently, she had not thought that he might require an explanation for her disappearance, nor had she thought, it seemed, of the mess in which her disappearance would leave him. He had quarrelled with Simona because of her. He had stood his ground and insisted that he would not abandon Hester, and now Hester had gone ahead and abandoned him.

It did occur to Robert, from time to time, that something else, something worse, might have happened to her, but then he would remind himself that Hester had been on her own for years, that she knew how to protect herself better than anyone else he knew, that she knew Liverpool better than anyone else he knew, and then he would go right back to being angry.

They had an unseasonably mild autumn, but in the middle of November, the temperature dropped overnight. Frost crept up onto the windows and sleet fell from the skies. This sudden arrival of winter, admittedly, gave Robert a few uneasy nights, as he lay awake wondering where Hester was sleeping. Then one Friday morning, a letter arrived which directed his thoughts away from Hester for a time.

The letter was from his sister Lesley, in Manchester. It started rather abruptly. Right after 'Dear Robert', Lesley asked if he had heard the news and went on to write, 'Maybe the word hasn't spread yet in Liverpool. The article was only published yesterday in the *Herald*. But it has named several mills and warehouses around Manchester as having bought Confederate cotton, including Cecil's own. Cecil is beside himself. I keep telling him he's not to blame, especially if Harold Fairbank lied to him about where he was sourcing his cotton, but he says that a friend of yours warned him about what Fairbank was doing, and that he ought to have listened to her. Who is this friend, Robert? Perhaps if she would be willing to bear witness, we could expose Fairbank. It's monstrous that someone like Cecil should have to take the blame when he had no idea what he was participating in. Fairbank is not even named in the article. Write back to me as soon as you can and let me know if your friend would be willing to help. Maybe she can even come to us in Manchester for a few days and we can discuss it there.'

Robert put down the letter, his mind reeling, to see that a customer had come in without his noticing and was waiting on the other side of the counter. "I beg your pardon," he said confusedly, and quickly served them. When they were gone, he called Marcus out from the kitchen to take his place. Then he donned his coat and hurried up the street to the bookseller's.

Mr. Moss was wrapped up against the elements, with a thick scarf covering the lower part of his face, meaning that his customary scowl was concealed and his aspect, therefore, was less forbidding than usual. Robert stopped by the stand, slightly out of breath, and asked, "Have you a copy of today's paper?"

"Good morning to you, too," the old man grunted in reply.

"Good morning. I'm sorry. I'm all in a heap this morning. I had a letter from Manchester." Robert paused as the bookseller passed him a copy of the Liverpool *Mail*. "Thank you." He leafed through it quickly. There were a few items on the American war, but nothing related to what Lesley had told him. He handed it back to Mr. Moss with another hasty thanks, and was already turning away when the man said,

"I suppose your letter must have from that girl."

"No, from my sister," Robert said distractedly, and then he turned back. "What girl?"

"The one who used to come around here all the time. She's in Manchester now, isn't she?"

"I don't know. I don't know where she is."Robert was staring at the bookseller. "How do you...?"

"She came here in quite a state one night, asking to stay with me. That was about a month ago, I reckon. She said she might to go to Manchester, and when I woke the next morning she was gone. Left only a note to say, 'thank you'."

"Can I see it?" Robert said at once.

"I don't know as I still have it." Mr. Moss's eyes had narrowed as he regarded him. Then he waved a hand at the books on the table in front of him. "Watch these and I'll go check."

He was gone for what seemed to Robert an unbearably long time. People walked up and down the lane, people passed in and out of the draper's shop and paused to look at the bookstand, before glancing uncertainly at Robert and passing on without buying anything. Finally Mr. Moss shuffled out of the shop again. Robert met him halfway and took the note from his gloved hand. It was in Hester's scratchy handwriting, and was only brief, but there was something at the end which caught his attention. "She says she's obliged to you for telling her about Fred," Robert said, looking up at Mr. Moss. "Who's Fred? That boy from the gang?"

"I don't know about any gang, but I know that she had a friend here who was bound for Manchester. Maybe she followed him there."

Robert nodded slowly and held up the note. "Can I keep this?"

"Well, I've no use for it."

Robert had no use for it either, not really, but at the very least it was something, and for the moment, it was the only explanation he was going to get for Hester's absence. Back at the bakery, he wrote an answer to his sister, telling her that the friend on whom she and Cecil had pinned their hopes was, unfortunately, gone away, and that she was not likely to come back.

CHAPTER TWENTY-SIX

Manchester was not like Liverpool. In Manchester, there were various parts of the city, such as the one that Hester had passed through on her first night, which were made up only of offices and warehouses. Any time that she had gone back to that part of the city since, she would be chased out on sight by a policeman or watchman. Worse still were the parts of the city where the manufacturers lived, in their big houses, and the shops and coffee-houses which they alone were allowed to patronise, and the neat city parks where they alone were allowed to walk. It had been different in Liverpool, where you might come to the end of one street and pass, just like that, from a poor district to a rich one. Hester had heard that Manchester was a workers' city. So, she found herself asking, where were all the workers?

For the first few weeks, she lived on the remainder of the four shillings that she had got for cutting her hair, one of which had been spent on her fare over. Soon she had found the working parts of town, though many of the mills that she passed had locked gates and boarded-up windows. In those that were still open, she would go in and make inquiries of the foremen or clerks. Some turned her away, but some obliged by checking their lists of workers and listening to her description of Fred Small, only to tell her afterwards that no such young man had come in looking for work. Hester was never really surprised by these answers. She knew that Fred was more likely to look for work in the old way, by hanging around the wealthy parts of town and pilfering what he could get, and seeing who he could get to help him, but in her search, she would leave no stone unturned. She decided that once she had visited all the mills in Manchester, she would go back to those other parts of town and look for Fred there, though she wasn't sure how she was going to do so without being chased out again.

No, Hester was not really surprised as day after day unfolded and brought no advance in her quest. What did surprise her was the kindness that was often shown her. She would walk through long terraces of workers' cottages that were pushed up so tightly together and so crammed with people and noise that she would almost feel sorry for their inhabitants, but it seemed that many of those inhabitants, seeing her wandering past the edges of their lives, felt sorry for her, too. Sometimes they would invite her in to share the warmth of their fire, or they would give her a sup of tea at their doorway. Sometimes they would chat with her and, hearing her Liverpool accent, would ask her if things were as bad over there as they were here. Hester would always say no, not just because it was true, but also because it was what they would be expecting and hoping for her to say.

One night, sitting on the step of an open kitchen door with a cup of tea beside her, Hester read *The Little Mermaid* again by the light of the coal fire blazing inside, while behind her she could hear the busy noise of a family settling in for the evening. Once or twice she would stop her reading to listen to the family. She gathered from what she overheard of their conversation that the children were all working half-days and going to school in the mornings. One of the boys, whom she judged to be around Fred's age, was asking why he couldn't throw over his lessons and start working full-time, since that was what all his friends were doing. It made Hester smile. She didn't finish the book, in part because she was thus distracted and in part because, after a time, when she tried to read the print, spots of light would come across her vision to blot it out. They would disappear once she blinked, but they kept coming back.

There were many things that Hester Grace couldn't forget about her past, and most of them had to do with Robert, but one image that returned to her more often than any other was that of the young, bruised face of Fred Small, when he had told her he wouldn't be bothering her or Robert anymore. Hester had let him walk away that night. She had turned him away when he had needed her most, and here in Manchester people had been kind to her when they might just as easily have turned her away. She would do everything she could, she resolved, to earn that kindness.

CHAPTER TWENTY-SEVEN

L esley replied to Robert's letter a few days later
saying that she was sorry to hear that he had
lost touch with his friend, and asking if he had
any ideas as to where that friend might have gone? Robert
debated writing back to tell her that Hester might be in
Manchester, and finally decided against it. For one thing,
he wasn't sure if it was true, and for another, even if it was
true, the boy, Fred, was the only clue he had as to where
Hester might be found, and that wasn't much of a clue at
all, since it would be no easier to find two kids on the
down-and-out in that vast city than it would be to find
one, especially since it was clear that neither of them
wanted to be found, so he left Lesley's letter unanswered.

One evening after he had finished work, he set out for
West Derby Road. He had arranged to meet Simona
Fairbank at a park near her aunt's house, and he half-

expected her not to turn up. But when he came in through the gates, he saw that she had arrived before him. She was waiting under the bare branches of an oak, and she turned towards him as his footsteps crunched across the frost-tipped grass. She had her hands in a muff and wore a cloak of deep blue whose hem trailed the ground. Looking at him, she lowered the hood, to reveal her rich gold-brown hair, arranged in perfect ringlets.

Robert doffed his cap and thanked her for coming. "I thought it would be better to meet you somewhere other than Canning Place, in case your father objected."

"You thought right," she said, calmly. "My father would be quite unhappy if he knew I was meeting you here, since he is still under the impression that you have a mistress, and I'm afraid nothing that I have said can convince him otherwise."

Robert winced a little at the words.

"But that would not be his sole objection," she went on. "He and my aunt are very busy arranging a match for me, you see. It's to be with a Mr. Forster. He owns a gas-works in town. I have seen him once at a party and I must say I did not dislike his looks."

"That sounds very fine," said Robert, after a painful silence. The silence stretched on, Miss Fairbank was looking at him, evidently expecting him to say something more. Finally she broke it herself, saying briskly,

"Let's walk. It's too cold to stand still."

"Yes," said Robert, falling into step beside her as he put his cap back on. "You're right, of course."

They started down the deserted path. As they walked, Robert glanced at Miss Fairbank's profile, just as he had done once before. It was as perfect now as it had been then, with her gold-tipped lashes, her button nose, her long sweep of white neck. Here she was beside him, he reminded himself, and here they were alone together. Her arm was nearly brushing his. With each step they took, the swing of her skirts would lightly graze his trousered leg. He noticed all of it. Whatever had blossomed between them in October, it was still there. Robert could feel it. In her presence, his heartbeat had quickened a little, his cheeks felt a little warmer, and he felt a bit unsteady. But was that all that he had felt, back then? He didn't know, but he had an idea that it must have been more. He distinctly remembered sitting with his head in his hands and noticing the fevered rush of his thoughts as though they were those of a stranger. *I feel like I'm going mad*, he had said to Hester, and she had answered – what had she answered again?

"I wasn't going to come," Miss Fairbank said, interrupting his reverie. "And if you'd sent her to ask me to meet you here, I certainly wouldn't have. But since you sent your apprentice instead..." She glanced towards him. "I'm sure you understand."

"Yes," Robert said, swallowing. "Well, the truth is, I couldn't have sent the message by Hester even if I had wanted to. She's gone."

"Gone?"

"She has left Liverpool. I think. She disappeared about a month ago. It was on the very same day that you and I last spoke, in fact."

"And she didn't tell you where she was going? You have not heard from her since?"

"No."

They walked on for another minute in silence. "I can't say I'm sorry," Miss Fairbank said at length, "since I didn't like her being around you so often, when her feelings were so clear."

"And as I told you before," said Robert, raising his eyes to the white, wintry sky, "you are mistaken if you think Hester's feelings for me were anything more than..."

"I will not hear this again. I can't answer for your feelings, but I can answer for hers. Why, she might have –" Miss Fairbank stopped herself.

"What? What were you going to say?"

"She might have been carted off to the police station that day when my father brought her to his office, if I hadn't spoken up for her. He was convinced she was a spy for

Cecil Locksmith. And she was going to stay silent. She was going to let him believe that she was a spy, rather than betray your secret. Our secret."

"It's a very good thing that you did defend her, then. And I'm grateful to you, as I'm sure she is, too." Robert glanced sidelong at her. "But what you speak of, her silence, that was just the act of a friend."

"If you insist on believing that, then I don't see any use in contradicting you." Miss Fairbank's tone softened then. "But I do hope that she has not gotten herself into trouble."

Robert sighed. He sensed her glance towards him. "Are you worried about her?"

"Yes," he said after a moment. "I heard recently that she might be in Manchester, and she does not know that city. She has spent her whole life in Liverpool. I am a little worried."

Miss Fairbank was silent. They had reached the end of the path and doubled back now. Robert went on, "But I didn't ask you here today to talk about Hester."

"Oh?"

"I was wondering if you had heard anything about the businessmen in Manchester who have been criticised for buying cotton grown by slaves. My brother-in-law is one of them, and as you can imagine, he's quite distressed, since your father assured him that his cotton was sourced elsewhere."

"My father has sourced his cotton from India and Egypt for some years now," Miss Fairbank said at once. "I believe I have told you this before."

"But if that's the case, then why has Cecil's warehouse been named as one of the businesses profiting from this supply? The whispers have to have come from somewhere. That is, where there's…"

"… where there's smoke, there's fire? Was that what you were going to say?" Miss Fairbank came to a sharp stop on the path, and he stopped too. She was staring at him. "So this was why you summoned me here? To tell me that my father is a liar?"

"I just want to know the truth," Robert said after a moment. "It is right and natural for you to defend your family, of course, just as it is right and natural for me to defend mine. My brother-in-law's reputation is at stake."

"I must correct you there, Mr. Burrows. Your brother-in-law's reputation will likely not be much harmed by this, as, in fact, there are many men in this kingdom who do not share his scruples about importing from the Confederacy. But my father is a man of conscience, just as your brother-in-law is. He would not accept cotton grown by slaves. I told you before that my father always consults me on matters of business, did I not? Well, I can assure you that if he ever did such a thing, I would be the first to know about it."

"But that's just what I'm wondering," Robert said hastily. "Forgive me, but is it not possible that there might be some parts of your father's business that he conceals from you?"

Miss Fairbank put up her hood, but he had seen the flash of doubt in her eyes. "I will forgive you, Mr. Burrows, for asking such questions, since it is, as you say, in service of the truth. But summoning me here under false pretences is unpardonable."

"False pretences?"

She rounded on him. "What else do you call it, when you lead a person to believe a thing that is not true? Perhaps you ought to think about that before accusing other people of lying."

"I didn't –" Robert started, but she left him mid-sentence, stalking off and out of the park.

Her anger surprised him. He could understand why having Hester stay with him, and having the fact known by her servants, would have made her angry. Her pride had been at stake in such a question, after all. But on this occasion, Miss Fairbank's anger seemed to have issued less from wounded pride than, Robert hesitated to think it, but a broken heart. She had evidently expected the meeting to go very differently. She had watched him so closely when she had said that about being as good as engaged to Mr. Forster, but here was what Robert couldn't understand. What did she expect him to do, when faced with such a rival? Robert had all the disadvantage in this question, and she had the advantage. She was the first woman that he had ever loved, while he had already been thrown over, it seemed, for a man who could offer her much more. Was he expected to keep fighting for her, doggedly, when he was given so little encouragement?

Robert took his time walking home, turning over their conversation in their head. Could it be the case, that he had arranged the meeting with her under false pretences? Had she been expecting a confession of love from him? Surely, he thought, he had shown his love in many ways. He had stood outside her father's office every day for a week, just waiting for the chance to speak to him. He had written that letter, and then, when Miss Fairbank had asked him to turn Hester out of his life, he had –

With a flush of confusion, Robert recalled it. He had said no, so perhaps his pursuit of her had not been as ardent as he had thought. But then, she couldn't have expected him to give way in all things. She couldn't have expected him to abandon his friends, or his principles. Could she have? A line had to be drawn somewhere. He was not her slave, and, just as that last thought struck him, the sounds of a commotion brought him back to the present.

The sun had set by now, but he was walking so slowly that he had not yet left the surrounds of West Derby Road. Now, from up ahead, out of the growing darkness, came a cry. "Thief! Thief!" Robert heard running footsteps coming straight towards him. As a skinny figure in a top hat and frock coat came into view, Robert moved quick as a flash to trip him up. The boy hit the pavement with a yelp and, in an instant, was wriggling to his feet again, but Robert caught the boy around the shoulders, and had a firm grip on him when two young gentlemen appeared, out of breath, to thank him profusely.

"We're in your debt, sir," said the first. "He plucked my pocket watch right out of my hand."

"And those clothes he's wearing are likely stolen, too," said the second, casting a doubtful eye over the boy's attire.

Robert made the boy hand back the pocket watch, but when the gentlemen suggested calling the watchman, he said, "If you please. I know this boy, and there's not much harm in him. He gave back your watch, after all, didn't he?"

"Yes," said the first gentleman, exchanging a glance with his friend, "But if he hadn't been caught…"

"But he was caught, so that settles the question, doesn't it?" Robert looked steadily from one to the other, until they relented, walking off together. The boy had, by now, gone still in Robert's grip, and it was quite easy to turn him around so that they were facing each other.

"Well," said Robert after a moment, "One good turn deserves another, don't they say? So maybe you can answer something for me. Where is Hester, and why aren't you in Manchester with her?"

CHAPTER TWENTY-EIGHT

One day, after Hester had spent her last sixpence in an alehouse, less to enjoy the taste of the brew than to warm herself by the fire, she knew that she could not put it off any longer. Her quest was far from over. There were over a hundred mills in Manchester, and she had only searched about half that number, if even that, but now that she had run out of money, she was going to have to find work. She had a slim chance of doing so, since she spent most of her nights in the streets and didn't have much opportunity of making herself clean or presentable. Every now and then she would pass a pump, and if she could bear the cold, she could clean her face, at least. But the rest of her got dirtier and tattier. She had found a pair of boots, but they were too big for her, and at night when she took out her feet, she would see large, blackened blisters on her feet. There were not many places in this town, she knew, that would take her on. But somewhere had to.

Just as she was thinking that, Hester became aware that she was being watched by somebody. She looked up to see that a woman was standing beside her table in the alehouse had been standing beside her table for some time, so it seemed, for she seemed to have settled into her position, one hand on her hip and her head cocked to one side as she regarded Hester.

"You look a sight, love," the woman said when their eyes met.

"I'm all right, thanks," said Hester, pretending to take a sip from her cup even though it was empty.

"You from Liverpool?"

Hester didn't reply. She knew what the woman wanted, or at least she had some idea. Now that Hester had been in Manchester about a month, her hair had started to grow out a bit and it was harder to hide herself, especially when her cap was off.

"Come with me and I'll help you get cleaned up," the woman said, smilingly.

"No, thanks." Hester stared into the inside of her cup.

"You'll have a bed for the night," the woman went on. "A hot meal."

Not trusting herself to speak now, Hester just shook her head from side to side, as vigorously as she could. She did not look up until she was sure the woman had gone, and then, feeling the eyes of the other patrons on her, she scrambled out of her chair and pulled her cap down low over her forehead as she left.

At the end of that day, having been turned out of every shop, factory, and mill that she had stepped into looking for work, or looking for Fred, or both, Hester found herself huddled in the shelter of a brick wall at the end of a blind alley. Here the wind was not so cruel, but still she was shaking all over, and something light and wet was falling on her head. She squinted up and saw that it was snow.

A hot meal, the woman in the alehouse had said, and a bed for the night. Hester knew the price for such things, her pride, her virtue, but she was beginning to think she might be willing to pay it. She wondered, if she went back now, whether the woman would still take her. She racked her brains and tried as hard as she could to remember the name of the alehouse. When no name came forth, she decided that she would just retrace her steps that day and keep her eye out for the familiar facade of the place.

CHAPTER TWENTY-NINE

Fred Small spent some time insisting that his name was not Fred Small, that he had never seen Robert before in his life, and that he had never heard of anyone by the name of Hester Grace, but at length, when the watchman's lantern came bobbing up the street, Fred became rather more forthcoming.

"Who's there?" called the watchman, and Robert raised his eyebrows at Fred.

"Very well," said the boy, in an undertone. "I know Hester."

They ducked off the pavement and down a side-lane before the watchman could come any closer, and as they hurried along, Fred told Robert, breathlessly, about how, when his friends had been arrested, it had become necessary for him to disappear for a while, and so he had spread the word that he was gone to Manchester, and he changed his name while he was at it.

"I'll still call you Fred, if that's all right," said Robert, shortly. "You know that Hester has gone there to look for you?"

"I'm sure I don't have any idea why she should do such a thing," Fred snorted.

Robert wondered if this boy always spoke in such an affected way. "Maybe because you're friends? Maybe because she was worried about you?"

"Oh, good sir, she never cared a jot for me. In fact, I imagine that the only person Hester Grace has ever cared about, besides herself, is you."

To meet, twice in one day, with the same opinion from two vastly different quarters was too much for Robert, and he tugged Fred to a halt with a grip on his sleeve. "You're wrong. She *was* worried about you. Here." With his free hand, he rummaged around for the note that he still carried in his coat pocket, and finally found it, holding it out to Fred. "You can read, can't you?"

"I should say so," retorted the boy, with a lift of his chin, and he looked over the note that Hester had written to Mr. Moss, mouthing along with the words. When he reached the end, he just shrugged his skinny shoulders and handed the note back to Robert. "Well. It's a pity that things got mixed up in this way, but I suppose there's nothing to be done now."

"What?" said Robert, astounded. "She went to Manchester to find you, and that's all you have to say?"

"Did I ask her to do such a thing?" Fred raised his eyebrows. "And she ought to know better. She and I were never friends, nor did we ever pretend to be. At the most we were compatriots, and then only for a brief amount of time."

"Compatriots," Robert repeated softly, with a shake of his head.

"Might I go now?" Fred gave an experimental tug on his sleeve. "I have told you everything that I know, and I'm afraid I have other demands on my time."

Robert let Fred Small go. Then he walked back to Cobbler's Lane, in more of a hurry now than he had been before. He was thinking of trains and of the great chimneys of Manchester. So it was quite a shock when he came upon his own sister, who ought to have been in Manchester, waiting at the doorstep of his bakery.

"You didn't answer my letter," said Lesley Locksmith, after they had embraced, "so I thought I'd better come myself and help you find your friend. Where have you been all this time?"

"Come inside and get warm," was Robert's response. He thought it wiser to wait until his sister had rested and eaten before he told her that she had had a wasted trip, and that, in fact, they would be going back to Manchester first thing tomorrow morning.

CHAPTER THIRTY

It was some time since Robert Burrows had been back to Manchester. He went there every Christmas, but only at Lesley and Cecil's insistence, and he never stayed for long. Before Lesley had married Cecil, she and Robert had worked in Manchester for a few years, and they had lost their younger brother to illness there. They had been still children back then, and little Sammy the youngest and sweetest of all of them, but his lungs had not survived the carding-rooms of Manchester's mills. When he thought about it, he didn't know how she could bear to live there now. It wasn't as though Liverpool had been all sunshine and light by comparison, but at least Liverpool was their city. To Robert, it seemed only right that one should suffer a little in one's own hometown. To suffer in a strange place, though...

"Are you sure that Hester really is in Manchester?" Lesley asked him now. She was sitting across from him in the second-class carriage and yawned over every second word. It had been Lesley's wish to get a train at a more comfortable hour of the morning, a wish which her brother had cruelly denied, to use her words, and so here they were on the seven o'clock train, speeding off to Manchester.

"I'm not sure of anything," Robert responded, leaning back against his seat and rubbing his hands over his face. "Not anymore."

Lesley was apparently unmoved by his despondency. "She might have changed her mind and decided not to go after all. Or she might have been prevented from going. Maybe she couldn't make the fare. There are so many things that might have happened and you're jumping to the first conclusion you can think of."

"If she was still in Liverpool, then why would she stay away from the bakery for so long?"

"From what you have told me," Lesley said slowly, "it sounds as though she might have had a few reasons for staying away."

Robert knew where this was going. "Whatever you're thinking, you're mistaken."

"Do you know what I'm thinking, then?"

"I know what everyone thinks. And I know they're wrong. Hester and I…" Robert shook his head.

"You've never thought of her that way?" Lesley said quietly.

"No."

"But, all the same, maybe she has thought of you. Think of all the things she's done."

"That's a point, actually." Robert leaned forward. "If Hester was in love with me, why would she have carried messages between me and Miss Fairbank?" He shook his head firmly. "I know what love looks like."

"Do you?"

Robert looked at his sister, at her brown hair plaited around the crown of her head, touched here and there with grey, at the deep shadows under her eyes. "Well, what do you know about it?" he retorted. "You've only ever loved Cecil."

"You only have to fall in love once to know what it's like," Lesley said, with one of those little, superior laughs that Robert despised. Married couples dealt exclusively in such laughs, it seemed. Ignoring it, he pressed on,

"And she told me to try again with Miss Fairbank when I was on the point of giving up. Why would she have done that if she was in love with me? It doesn't make any sense."

"Wouldn't you do it? If the person you loved could be happy with someone else, wouldn't you let them go?"

"No," said Robert, appalled, and his sister gave another laugh. This one was slightly less superior, at the very least.

"Well, not everyone's like you, Rob. Anyway, I'm going to close my eyes for a while. You know I didn't get enough sleep last night."

"Because I made us get up early," Robert finished, rolling his eyes. "I know. I'll wake you up when we get there."

CHAPTER THIRTY-ONE

Cecil and Lesley lived on Hope Street, in a house that had belonged to Cecil's aunt before her death, and which they could no longer really afford. Over the last few years, they had to dismiss most of the servants, and now kept only a cook and a maid. To Robert, the fact of having any servants at all was still something he couldn't get his head around, since he had lived his whole life up until now without them and was content to go on doing so, but this was just one of the many ways in which his sister had changed since her marriage. Lesley hadn't grown up in a house with servants either, but that didn't stop her from complaining now about how hard it was to find good help these days, and how their maid was always idling when she should be working, and how the cook always overcooked meat with the result, apparently, of killing all its flavour. That she, Cecil, and their children could still afford to eat meat more than once a week already put them far above most families in Manchester, and Liverpool besides, but Robert knew better than to mention this to Lesley, as it would only set her off on a list of all the luxuries that she and Cecil had had to give up since his business had fallen on hard times.

At any rate, once Lesley had woken up a bit after their train journey, she was very helpful in drawing up a list of all the possible places where Hester might be found, so that Robert couldn't really fault her if she spoke a little sharply to the maid when the latter forgot to set the table for breakfast. After they had eaten, Lesley and Robert set out to visit some of these places. There was the workhouse on the south bank of the Irk, set at a height above one of the workers' quarters. They crossed a bridge over dark, slimy waters and entered the building in silent dread, leaving as soon as they had ascertained that there was no 'Hester Grace' on the register. Then there were various charitable societies to visit, dotted all around the city. Lesley and Robert walked everywhere, and that there was one point, at least, where his sister had not changed. When they had been growing up in Liverpool, she used to walk miles and miles without even noticing, and now she was the very same. After a time, Robert found that he was the one who was winded, and luckily Lesley spared him the embarrassment of admitting as much by suggesting they stop in an inn for something to eat.

They sat by the windows and watched as grey flakes of snow began to whirl outside the glass. "There are a few more places on my list," Lesley said, "But we might not get to them all today. How long are you planning to stay?"

"As long as I need to," Robert said, staring out the window. He sensed his sister's swift glance but did not look around.

"What about the bakery?"

"Marcus can manage. It'll be good for him. He'll be seventeen soon. Nearly time for him to start running his own place."

Lesley was silent for a moment. Still not dragging his eyes from the window, Robert took a sip from his glass of beer. His sister said, "Of course, in this weather, you know it's possible that she might have..."

"Don't say it," Robert told her, so sternly that she dropped the subject, but that evening, Cecil ended up bringing it up anyway. After returning from work, he immediately set about listing all the places that Lesley might have missed.

"There's the hospital, and the morgue. The pauper's burial ground behind the workhouse."

"But if she was buried there, it would have been anonymously," Lesley said, with all the calm of someone who was discussing an absolute stranger.

"Try a few of the Friendly Societies, then. They often organise whip-rounds for paupers' funerals, to give them a proper burial."

Robert got up from the table and walked out of the dining room. He went to bed without speaking to either Lesley or Cecil, and the next morning they both apologised to him.

"You know it's just something we have to consider," Lesley said, standing behind Robert with her arm around his shoulders. They were sitting in the drawing room, their updated list on the writing desk in front of them.

"I have considered it," Robert growled, though he didn't shrug off his sister's touch. "What else do you think I consider when I think of her wandering alone here? But she isn't, not yet. She can't be. There's still time, if we hurry up and find her."

CHAPTER THIRTY-TWO

Hester hadn't found the alehouse with the woman, try as she might. The snow had got too thick, and she had been unable to retrace her steps. She had ended up sneaking under a gap in the wall enclosing an abandoned mill, and breaking one of the windows to climb in. Blood was pooling over her knuckles as she pushed open a door, but she was so cold that she barely noticed, and she hurried down the stairs to the basement. The boilers there evidently had not been in use for some time, but they still carried some residual heat, and Hester curled up as close as she could get to one of them. She spent a succession of nights like that, begging or stealing food during the day. Then, one evening, she saw through the gap in the wall that the gates to the mill stood open, and that several gentlemen were walking about in the yard. She knew that she could not slip past them unnoticed, and that she would have to find somewhere else to sleep that night.

Her quest was now one of mere survival. It had dawned on her, on one of those winter nights of howling wind and swirling snow, that even if she found Fred, she could be of no help to him. She could not even help herself. If he was in trouble, then so was she. That was how Hester began to think. At least, that was how she thought when she had the energy to think. So, on the night when she lost her sleeping spot, she went around from tavern to tavern and started asking everyone whom she met if they knew where Cecil Locksmith's warehouse was.

Cecil was the only person she knew in Manchester. He had been kind to Hester once before, and she knew he would be kind to her now, if she could only find him. She hadn't wanted to stoop to such a measure on first arriving here, of course. But now she was far away from all feelings of pride, and any aversion to charity had long since disappeared. Once, back in Liverpool, Hester remembered thinking that she wanted to die, looking into the grey waters of the Mersey and wondering if they would be deep enough to drown her. These days, though, when death was so close to her, lurking around the next street-corner, in the cold breath of the wind as it touched her face, Hester felt a fire in her veins. She wanted to keep living. She would do whatever it took to make sure she did. She had very nearly stooped so low as to sell herself. Asking for charity could not be as bad as that.

It took a lot of blank faces and slammed doors before Hester could ascertain that Mr. Locksmith's warehouse was in Ancoats, to the north-east of the city, but for Hester, who didn't know where she was, this information did not count for much until she had found out, through asking around a bit more and observing street signs, that she was in the south, in Moss Side. That name made her smile a bit, as she remembered her old friend Mr. Moss, such a long way away and such a long time ago, but she had still had the book he had given her. Yes, and she would never let it out of her hands.

Hester walked for a few days to get to where she needed to be. She got to where the buildings were blacker, and the streets were positively choked with smoke. Yet they were utterly deserted, at least until a strange horn blew in the distance and suddenly people began to stream out of doors from all directions. She was jostled right and left. "Move along, now, girl," a few of the kinder passersby said. The rest uttered words that made Hester wince on instinct, though such words had no real power to hurt her anymore.

She was eventually pointed in the right direction to get to the building that housed Mr. Locksmith's warehouse. Like many such buildings in Manchester, it was enclosed by a wall. She went up to ring the bell at the gate. When the foreman came down, she told him her name and that she wished to see Cecil Locksmith, but he just said the same thing to her as the people in the street had done. "Move along, now."

"But I know him," Hester called through the gate to the man's retreating back, or at least she tried to call. Her voice came out all reedy and thin. It was like something in a nightmare, trying to tell someone something urgent and finding that your voice made no sound. "If you tell Mr. Locksmith my name, Hester Grace…"

The man disappeared into the building. Hester walked a little way from the gate and then sank down with her back to the wall. She stayed like that even as the cold began seep into her from below, even as the snow started falling from above. It wasn't that she didn't feel or notice those things; it was just that she knew her legs would not carry her any further. She squinted at the snow in front of her eyes, her eyes getting narrower and narrower as she struggled to keep them open.

CHAPTER THIRTY-THREE

It had been a week. Marcus had sent an anxious letter from Liverpool asking when 'Mr. Burrows' would return as things were very busy in the bakery and he had missed a delivery yesterday because he was attending to a customer and now there wasn't enough flour and did Robert know where he could get some, just to last them until next week when the delivery came again? Robert wrote back with very clear instructions, his left hand pinching the space between his eyebrows as his right hand moved across the page. Lesley began to hint that it might be time for them to pay another visit to a few of those Friendly Societies, to see if they had helped fund any funerals in the last week of someone matching Hester's description. "She mightn't have been able to give her name, you see, dear." Robert knew that if his sister was calling him 'dear,' she must be very seriously worried. Once again, he waved away the suggestion, but that night, lying in bed in Cecil and Lesley's guest room, he listened to the wind howling outside and thought to himself that Hester couldn't possibly still be alive.

"Why on earth did you let her go to Manchester?" Cecil asked on one occasion, after he and Robert had been to visit a few mills in Ancoats to see if Hester's name was, by any chance, on any of the employee lists. Cecil said that he would check more mills with Robert when he had more time. Robert wanted to scream that there was no time, but even he knew there was not much point in checking employee lists. There was no work for anybody these days, least of all for an orphan girl from Liverpool who had no references.

"Let her go?" Robert repeated.

"Didn't I tell you to take care of her?" Cecil said, but then he must have seen something in Robert's face that made him regret his words, for he clapped a hand on his brother-in-law's back and added, "Of course you did your best."

Cecil grew increasingly distracted with each day that passed, for he had a shareholders' meeting coming up which would decide the fate of his company. It seemed that he and Lesley could talk of little else. Even the children spoke about it in anxious whispers in the landing, though Mary, at seven, was not able to pronounce the word 'shareholder' and Sam, at ten, did not quite grasp the meaning of the word, though he certainly thought he did.

"Uncle Rob?" said Mary, coming up to him in the hall one morning when he was about to head out, for the first time alone, as both Cecil and Lesley were busy that day. "You wished Daddy luck for his meeting later, didn't you?"

"Yes," said Robert, ruffling her hair. "I did, don't you worry."

"And, Uncle Rob." She beckoned him closer and looked at him seriously. "I asked everyone in school about your friend, but no one knows her. Isn't her name Esther Grace? I wish my last name was Grace and not Locksmith. Locksmith is so ugly."

"Thank you," said Robert, giving his niece a hug. "It was good of you to ask."

Alone, Robert found that his sister's hints had had their effect after all, for he bent his steps to the building that housed the nearest Friendly Society. They had not come across anyone of Hester's description, and neither had the next society that he visited, but the third society, located in Hulme, told Robert that they had helped fund the funeral just the other day of a girl who had died of exposure: This girl, they said, had been young, somewhere between sixteen and twenty, with dark hair. "What colour were her eyes?" Robert asked. When they told him 'brown,' he said, "Oh no!" and sat right down.

They couldn't tell him the name, for they said the girl had been unconscious when she was taken up and brought to the hospital, and she had not lived much longer after that. As Robert left the building, emerging into a cold, bright, grey world, he wondered if it would be better to pretend as though the last hour had never happened. He needn't tell Lesley and Cecil. He could go on searching for Hester. For perhaps the girl hadn't been her. There was still a chance.

Later, when Robert tried to remember the rest of that day, and where he had gone, it was all a horrible blank to him. He supposed that he must have walked quite a distance, for the next thing he remembered after walking out of the Friendly Society in Hulme was waiting for Cecil outside his warehouse in Ancoats, at nightfall. The foreman had let him into the inner yard and offered him a place inside to wait if he liked, but Robert stayed where he was, outside, pacing up and down and clapping his hands together every now and then to keep them warm. This was nothing, he kept telling himself, nothing compared to what she must have gone through. He hoped that it had been easy at the end. He had heard that it was like falling asleep. He hoped that she had felt like that, like she was closing her eyes on a cruel world to wake up in a better one.

Light flooded across the yard sometime later, and a crowd of gentlemen emerged, evidently the shareholders. Robert watched them as the foreman showed them out through the gate. Cecil was the last to emerge from the building, and he walked slowly over the sludgy ground. His face was like old paper.

"It's finished," he told Robert when he reached him.

"Finished?" Robert repeated. "You don't mean…"

"The shareholders have all withdrawn. Since my warehouse cannot get a sufficient supply of cotton anymore, they've all sold their shares. Tomorrow I'm going to have to dismiss a hundred workers."

Cecil walked to the gate, Robert at his heels. "Goodnight, Mr. Locksmith, Mr. Burrows," said the foreman as he showed them out onto the street.

"Goodnight," the two men echoed.

"I'll even have to dismiss him," Cecil said to Robert when they were out of earshot of the man. "And he knows it, too. I could hear it in his voice."

"What are you and Lesley going to do?"

"Oh, we'll manage for now. We have a little put by, so we'll give Sam and Mary a good Christmas, in any case. And after that…" Cecil glanced to the side as they passed a beggar, who was barely distinguishable as more than a dark shape against the wall, and then he went on, "Who knows."

"There's something that I have to tell you, too," said Robert, who had not seen the beggar. All he knew was that he felt slightly sick, and his voice sounded oddly loud in the cold, still night. It had stopped snowing some time ago. Robert felt Cecil's gaze on him but found he couldn't go on.

"Is it do with Hester?" said Cecil after a long pause, and Robert nodded. "And it's not good news, by your looks."

Robert nodded again, so that his head sunk to his chest. Cecil reached out and put a hand between his shoulder-blades, nodding every now and then as Robert, in halting tones, related the results of his visit to the Friendly Society. "Of course, there's a chance it mightn't have been her," Robert finished, and glanced up to see if his hope was reflected in Cecil's eyes. It wasn't.

"I think," said Cecil, heavily, "Robert…"

But he never got to finish his sentence, for from somewhere behind them came the sound of a thump, and they both turned around to see that the beggar had slipped from their position by the wall and was lying on the cold, hard ground. Robert was the first to rush forward. He knelt in sludge and cushioned the beggar's dark head with one hand, doing his best to lift him back into a sitting position with the other. "Cecil, help," he said, but his brother-in-law was hesitating beside him.

"Maybe it's best to leave him, Robert," said Cecil. "We should be getting home."

"He's still breathing," Robert responded, and then, as soon as the beggar's head was a safe distance from the ground, he let go of it and tried to get him sitting steady by putting an arm around his shoulders. The beggar's head lolled, and his cap fell off, and suddenly Robert could see a face before him, a face covered in dirt, wrought with exhaustion, and pale as the grave, but there was the same high forehead, the same black waves of hair, though cruelly sheared now and having grown back a little uneven. The eyes were closed, but between the dark lashes were flashes of white.

"Hester!" Robert heard Cecil's intake of breath behind him as soon as he had uttered the name. "Am I dreaming?" he croaked over his shoulder to his brother-in-law. "Is it her?"

"I can't tell," Cecil said, coming forward and easing into a crouch beside Robert. "If it is, she looks very different."

Robert touched the beggar's face and their eyes opened, brown and solemn, staring into Robert's, and then he knew that it was her and he started saying over and over, "Oh, thank You, God." He pulled her in so that her head was cradled against his chest. Cecil scrambled to his feet and ran for help. Hester's eyes closed again as though the scene was too much for her, but seconds later, a feeble hand came up to graze Robert's shoulder, and he heard her say, quietly, "I knew you would find me."

But they very nearly hadn't found her, and over the next few days, Robert often thought of how close they had come to missing her. When Cecil asked his foreman, he said that she had come calling at the warehouse hours before, and that of course he hadn't let her in. She must have been waiting out there in the snow for at least half a day. Before that, who knew how far she had wandered, what she had lived on. Very far, and not very much, were the answers suggested by her frightening thinness and the blisters on her feet. Robert often thought, too, of the girl who had died, and whose fate Hester could have followed.

The surgeon made frequent visits to the house. He kept saying how lucky Hester had been, and that some rest and nourishment would soon mend her, but there was one awful night where all those words seemed to spin away into nothing. Robert, now sleeping in the spare bed behind the scullery that had once been a servant's room, in the days when there had been a whole retinue of servants in Hope Street, the days which his sister seemed to long for, woke with a jolt and a feeling of something wrong. He felt his way through the darkness, bumped his head on a low doorframe, and finally lit a candle.

He climbed up the dark stairs to the guest room, laying a hand on the door for a minute before he went in, and just listening, but all he could hear was silence within. He opened the door and the light of the candle illuminated Hester in her bed, sleeping very soundly. Still uncertain, Robert approached the bed slowly. His sister and the maid had cleaned Hester up as soon as they had brought her home, and brushed out her hair, so she looked something like her old self, but there were still cuts and bruises all over her that told the story of her ordeal more plainly than anything else. Robert could see nasty scratches on her left knuckle, where her hand, gripping the edge of the blanket over her, had tightened into a fist. Then he looked again, at that clenched hand, and frowned. As he listened more closely, he started to notice that Hester's breathing sounded very shallow. With a chill of fear, he put down his candle on the end table and held a hand to her forehead. She had a raging temperature, and the dark hairs at her hairline were matted with sweat.

Robert did not waste time waking up the maid, Lesley, or Cecil. He ran for the surgeon himself, leaving the candle still burning by Hester's bedside. His sister scolded him later for such carelessness, pointing out that his running to fetch the surgeon wouldn't have done much good for Hester if the house had been burned down around her. Robert acknowledged the truth of this, but at the time, only one thing was running through his brain: the surgeon, the surgeon, the surgeon. He had just enough presence of mind to throw on a coat over his nightshirt, so that he wouldn't freeze to death as he ran from street to street, making his way to the surgeon's house in Deansgate.

The surgeon, once he was dressed and had his bag, took Robert back to Hope Street in his horse and trap, a mode of transport which, while admittedly quicker than running, did not seem nearly quick enough. When they got back, there was a light on in the house, and Lesley and Cecil, having been roused by the slam of the front door as Robert left, met them in the hall. Together, they all hurried up to the guest room, where Hester was lying still and quiet in bed, too still and too quiet, Robert could see now, and he hung back in the doorway with a hand over his mouth as the surgeon went to examine her. Lesley put an arm around Robert's shoulders and Cecil patted him on the back, and they murmured, alternately, words of comfort that had little meaning. How would Hester be 'all right' when she looked like that?

"We must not interfere with the natural course of the fever," pronounced the surgeon once he had adjusted Hester's position and instructed Lesley in rearranging the bedclothes to make her more comfortable. "Any outside attempt to violently expel the fever would be a shock that her body, exhausted as it now is, might not survive. I will return at dawn to see how she is. By then we will have a clearer idea of how things stand." He clapped Robert's shoulder in passing, and seconds later they heard the slam of the front door.

The surgeon had cautioned against violent attempts to expel the fever, but what started happening to Hester's body over the next few hours seemed violent enough on its own, without any outside interference. No longer was she still and silent in bed. She began thrashing around and talking nonsense, throwing back her blankets and shaking all over. "Fight it, Hester," Robert cried, as his sister went to readjust the blankets. "Fight it! You're strong enough!"

"She can't hear you, Robert," said Cecil gently. He had just returned from downstairs with the maid in tow, who was carrying a tray of tea for them. It was not light yet, but they were all in need of refreshment. Robert ignored the tray, ignored Cecil's words as he approached Hester's bed.

"Fight it," he said again, and then she responded, in a clear voice that was nothing like the fevered mumble of the last few hours,

"Robert."

Robert turned around to look at Cecil, Lesley, and the maid, his expression half-exultant, half-wondering. He knelt at Hester's side and found her clammy hand, pressing it gently with his own. "I'm here, Hester," he told her. "I'm right here with you."

"Robert," she said again, her eyes still closed but a relieved smile on her face. "I love you."

Robert turned around again. This time, it was his sister's turn to look exultant. "She doesn't know what she's saying," Robert said quickly. "She's delirious."

"Margaret, you can go," Cecil told the maid, whose eyes were now as wide as saucers as she beheld the scene before her. "We'll ring if we need you."

"I love you, Robert," Hester said again, as the door closed behind the maid, and Robert stared down at her sleeping face before releasing her hand. He tucked it back under the covers and walked slowly back to join Lesley and Cecil, whose silence spoke volumes.

"You should go get some sleep," Lesley told her brother sometime later. He had now pulled up a chair close to Hester's bedside, though he had not taken her hand this time, and he shook his head.

"I'm staying right here till the surgeon comes back. He'd better be on time."

Hester murmured some more nonsense and cried out a few times, but when the first strains of morning light filled the room, she was sleeping quietly once more. Robert didn't really know what to think, since this was the state in which he had first found her. He felt her forehead a few times and fancied that it was cooler, but he didn't know for sure. By now Lesley and Cecil had gone back to bed, and when the surgeon finally arrived, he was an hour late, full of apologies as he'd had a patient in Chorlton. He examined Hester very briefly and told Robert that there was nothing to worry about for the moment, that she had come through the crisis. Robert didn't really believe him, didn't want him to go away again so soon, and it was only because he was tired of Lesley's nagging that he eventually, sometime later, toddled back down to bed to sleep an uneasy sleep and to dream confused dreams.

Hester slept nearly all of the remaining time that Robert stayed in Manchester. He checked on her every now and then. In those moments that he sat by her, he hoped, selfishly, that she would open her eyes and talk to him, but not to say such things as she had said in the delirium of fever, such things as had confused and alarmed him. Still, he didn't want to have to say goodbye to her sleeping form, but the necessity for that goodbye soon came, forced upon him by another anxious letter from Marcus. Lesley and Cecil told Robert that Hester was not well enough to travel yet, and that she would stay with them for the time being. They reminded him that Christmas, and his next visit to Manchester, were not so far away.

CHAPTER THIRTY-FOUR

C oming back to life, it seemed, took time. In fact, it took longer than it had any right to take, or so Hester thought as the days bled from November into December. She longed to be out of bed and in the fresh air again but was told by everyone that she would have to wait a little longer. She had never spent so long enclosed within four walls, even during her time in Brownlow Hill, where they had always had daily airings in the exercise yards. These four walls were very nice and neat compared to those of the workhouse, and she was as comfortable as she could be, and sometimes the children of the house would come in and play games with her or read to her, or, whenever she felt up to it, she would read to them. For it was true that there were moments when waves of weakness would come over her after the slightest exertion, and when she would feel the wisdom of the general decision to confine her to bed.

When she was allowed, for the first time, to venture downstairs and sit an hour or two in the drawing room, that was something. From the window, she could see the activity of the streets, carriages and carts and interesting people, faces other than the six faces that she saw all the time: Mr. and Mrs. Locksmith, their children, and their two servants. When she was allowed to take her meals with everyone else, that was something, too. Hester had hated being served her meals in bed, and she could tell that the maid had hated it, too, but, unfortunately, she found that downstairs in the dining room, meals were still being served to her. At first, she would try to help where she could, passing around serving bowls and carrying empty dishes into the kitchen, but that just seemed to make everyone unhappy. The cook and the maid glared, and Mr. and Mrs. Locksmith exchanged glances and told Hester, gently, "You're our guest."

Hester didn't really know what it meant to be a guest. She thought, sometimes, that it meant certain things were expected of her, and yet no one would say what those things were. Often she had caught Mr. and Mrs. Locksmith looking at her strangely, and once or twice, through closed doors in hushed conferences that she hadn't meant to overhear, she had heard her name spoken. Mrs. Locksmith would often talk to her about Robert, too, asking her about when and how they had met and how long they had known each other. As Hester answered those questions, Mrs. Locksmith would listen with a look on her face as though she already understood everything.

Hester wondered if her secret was really as plain as all that, as if it were written all over her. She would have blushed for it, only she was past embarrassment now. Mostly she only felt gratitude, and a growing need to escape the four walls around her.

When she was allowed to help with putting up the Christmas decorations, that was another milestone. She rushed to the front door as Mr. Locksmith and some neighbourhood boys were carrying in the tree and asked if she might do something to help. They didn't notice her as they passed down the hall, and for a moment Hester stood by the open door, smelling the scent of pine-needles and savouring the cold rush of air on her face. Then Mrs. Locksmith emerged and pulled her away, saying that if she caught a chill now, it might be the death of her. Once the tree was put up, Hester was put in charge of the tinsel and even entrusted with fastening the angel to the top, but she was not to be allowed near any open doors.

About a week later, Hester's hosts sat her down in the study and asked her if she might do them a favour. She stared from Mr. to Mrs. Locksmith, wondering what favour she could possibly do for them, and whether they might not be just dressing something up as a favour in a kind consciousness of her need to be useful. Then she saw the anxious entreaty in their expressions, and she realised that whatever they were about to ask of her, they actually thought that there was a chance she might refuse it. They told her about the article that had been published in the

Herald, how Mr. Fairbank had been unmentioned in the report, and how they wished to set the record straight by pointing the blame where it really lay.

"Of course," she said, as soon as Mr. Locksmith had finished speaking. "Of course I'll speak to this man, the reporter."

Mr. Locksmith looked relieved, but his wife cast him a troubled glance before leaning forward in her chair. "Hester, we don't want you to think of this as some kind of payment for your being here, as our guest. You have every right to refuse to see this man."

"Thank you," said Hester, "But I know it's the right thing to do."

The next day, she set out with Cecil Locksmith in the early afternoon, and she felt the happiest she had felt in a long time. Even though she had to submit to a short carriage ride, – she was out, and moving again. Hester had never ridden in a carriage before, and she found it much bumpier and more jarring than she had found the train. Manchester seemed still as strange to her as ever, with its workers' quarters, factories, and mills all crowded to one side of town, while the great houses and spacious parks took up another. And it was in this latter part of town that the carriage set them down. Mr. Locksmith helped Hester out of the carriage, which was necessary not just because of her weakness but because she was unused to moving with such a volume of petticoats and skirts around her legs. They took small steps along the pavement, moving towards a handsome building with mullioned windows, which Mr. Locksmith told her was a hotel.

The clink of cutlery and the low buzz of voices greeted them as they passed through the dining room. It was nothing like the blare of noise Hester expected to hear in any place where a great many people were eating together. It made her uneasy, and in the flannel drawers which Mrs. Locksmith had insisted that she put on under her petticoat, she was already starting to feel overheated. They were shown into a private room, where the snowy linen and array of cutlery on the table only served to add to Hester's awe, and she was so confused when the liveried waiter came to their table that Mr. Locksmith ended up ordering for her. It was better after they had eaten and their dishes had been cleared away, because then the man sitting across from them began to ask questions.

Hester wondered if Mr. Locksmith might have said something to this reporter in advance of their meeting, because the latter's manner was so calm and reassuring that she quickly felt herself relax. He did not stare at her curiously, which was what she had dreaded. He did not look at her very much at all, in fact, though he listened carefully to what she told him about that night in Albert Dock, and only occasionally did he write something down in his notebook.

When she had finished relating how Mr. Fairbank had sent the man Farrell to take her to his office in the mistaken impression that she was a spy for Cecil Locksmith, the reporter smiled for the first time, though briefly, and remarked to Mr. Locksmith, "To suspect that he is surrounded by spies would certainly suggest that he has secrets to guard, and not just trade secrets, either."

Mr. Locksmith voiced his agreement, and the reporter, turning his attention back to Hester, asked, "You say that Mr. Fairbank thought that Mr. Locksmith was working with Byron Davies to discredit him?"

"Yes, sir, Byron Davies. That was the name he gave."

"Well, it's strange," said the reporter, glancing at Mr. Locksmith, "but Mr. Davies has been writing to our offices for quite some time with concerns about how the warehouse that he rented out to Mr. Fairbank was being put to use. He could never give us anything substantial, only conjecture. Now, however, well, perhaps Mr. Fairbank's fears about you and Mr. Davies's having a common enemy in him might not have been entirely unfounded."

"Will he go to prison?" Hester asked, struck by a sudden thought. "Mr. Fairbank, I mean?"

"Well, importing Confederate cotton is not illegal," said the reporter.

"Though it should be," Cecil added.

"As it happens, I am in agreement with you, Mr. Locksmith, but in fact, opinions are fairly divided on the question. Even in our own paper, since the war broke out, we have given fairly equal ground to both camps, those supporting the Union and those supporting the Confederacy. It is said by some, indeed, that the Union has embarked on this war to benefit their own domestic industries rather than out of any real interest in abolishing slavery." Turning back to Hester, the reporter went on, "But to answer your question, Miss Grace, Mr. Fairbank may be facing charges of fraud. He misrepresented the source of his cotton supply to Mr. Locksmith, and that is serious indeed."

Hester fell silent, looking down at the table. For the rest of the meeting, she was spared from answering any more questions, as Mr. Locksmith and the reporter went over various particulars regarding the article that would soon be published in the Manchester *Herald*. Finally, they got up and shook hands, and on their way out of the hotel, Mr. Locksmith told Hester,

"Well done. I'm sure you must know already how grateful Lesley and I are to you for agreeing to do this, and it could not have gone off better."

"I'm glad," said Hester, quietly, but she was thinking of what would happen when the article was published in a few days, when Miss Fairbank opened the paper to read about her father. "Mr. Locksmith, do you think that Robert will mind?"

"Mind?" Cecil repeated. "Why should he mind? He's been longing for this matter to be cleared up as much as we have." He sighed. "Hester, you don't know what a weight it is off my mind, knowing that I can face the world with a clean conscience, that I can hold my head up high and say that I have never betrayed those principles which ought to govern every man's existence."

"It was the right thing to do," Hester said again, though she felt less convinced of the sentiment this time.

"Quite so. Well, here's our carriage."

CHAPTER THIRTY-FIVE

One afternoon during his dinner hour, Robert Burrows put on his Sunday best and walked the half a mile from Cobbler's Lane to Canning Place. He hesitated for just a moment before stepping up to ring the doorbell. The butler who answered the door looked Robert up and down. "Yes, she is at home, sir," he said, when Robert asked for Miss Fairbank, "though I do not know if she is at liberty to receive guests at the moment. She has another engagement shortly. If you would like to leave your card..."

"I don't have a card, I'm afraid," Robert said pleasantly. "But I won't keep her from her next engagement."

"You may come in and wait, then, sir, if you like," said the butler after a moment, with the air of making a grand concession. "I shall see if she has time to speak with you."

He showed Robert into the parlour, which was so full of flowers that the smell was almost sickening.

Robert paced up and down, preferring to stand than to sit. The butler had not taken his coat, so he folded it over one arm and looked around to see if there was some surface he could place it on. The armchairs had very white doilies on them that he thought he'd better steer clear of. There might be space for it beside that vase of chrysanthemums.

"You."

The door, standing ajar, had been eased open without Robert noticing, and now he turned to behold Mr. Fairbank standing in the doorway. "You, sir, should know better than to call at this address," he said in a low voice, pointing at Robert. "After your conduct towards my daughter, entertaining that harlot in your shop."

"Papa, I have told you that was a misunderstanding." Miss Fairbank joined her father at the threshold. She was dressed today in soft pink, a warmer colour than Robert had ever seen her wear before, with her hair in its usual ringlets but arranged in a magnificent style above her head.

"Misunderstanding! My own servants told me of it. Simona, you are all too forgiving." Mr. Fairbank's voice moved away as his daughter steered him a little distance from the door, and Robert, who was still standing in the parlour, cap in hand, heard them argue for a few minutes in hushed voices. The occasional phrase reached his ears.

"… to aspire to you in the first place. He was already unworthy, even had his conduct not proven it…"

"But what harm can there be in his seeing me now, Papa? Now that everything is settled?"

Finally, Mr. Fairbank gave way, and Robert heard him stalking down the hall and up the stairs. A moment later, Miss Fairbank reappeared at the door, meeting Robert's gaze for the first time. In a manner unruffled and distantly friendly, she said, "I am sorry to have kept you waiting, Mr. Burrows."

"Not at all," said Robert, making a small bow, his coat nearly sliding off his arm in the process. "And I understand you have another engagement, so I shan't keep you long."

Miss Fairbank stepped sideways in through the door and then righted herself with a swing of her crinoline. She slid the door closed and was still smiling as she turned back to face Robert. "Will you sit down?"

"Er…" Robert cast a doubtful glance at the white doilies.

"Please sit," said Miss Fairbank, very kindly, and so he obeyed. She took the armchair opposite his, with a long table in between them, and folded her white hands in her lap. Since she seemed in no hurry to speak, Robert went first.

"I'm sorry to disturb you like this. I didn't want to arrange a meeting this time in case it gave the wrong impression."

As Miss Fairbank's blue eyes flashed dangerously, he finished, hastily, "I felt it my duty to warn you of something that will happen soon."

"Pray tell," said Miss Fairbank, sweetly, after Robert hesitated.

"Well, you see, I've had a letter from my brother-in-law, Cecil Locksmith, in Manchester. You'll recall..."

"Yes, Mr. Burrows, the name does ring a bell."

Swallowing, Robert went on, "Well, Cecil is to meet soon with a reporter from the Manchester *Herald*. It seems that there is new evidence against your father, to indicate that he did indeed lie about where he was sourcing his cotton."

"I see," said Miss Fairbank, after a painful pause.

"I wanted to warn you before the article comes out, as I'm sure the Liverpool papers will soon pick it up too and I didn't want it to come as a shock to you."

"I'm much obliged to you, Mr. Burrows, for such solicitude, though I'm sure it's not necessary. You see, I have found that it is better not to pay much attention to what the papers say. Half of what goes to print tends to be utter nonsense."

Robert nodded slowly, not because he agreed with the sentiment but simply because he did not know what else to do. "Well." He adjusted his grip on his coat. "Perhaps I'd better..."

"You're not leaving already?" she asked as he started to rise from his chair. "Really, Mr. Burrows, I know you might not be as familiar with such courtesies as we are, but I thought it generally known that when you call on a lady, you are expected to stay at least a quarter of an hour."

Robert's eyes were fixed on the door. He knew that only a few short steps would take him there and out of this sweet-smelling room, but he couldn't help it. He wrenched his eyes from the door and rested them on her again. She was still sitting, still smiling in that infuriating way.

"I'm sure you can understand," he said, "if I don't want to linger where I am not welcome. I am sorry if the actions of my brother-in-law, though they were actions which I think he was right to take, give you and your father pain."

"Is that all you are sorry for?" Miss Fairbank asked, the smile dropping from her face. "You are sorry if the actions of your brother-in-law give me pain? Have I understood you right?"

Robert stared down at her, and then began to move for the door, saying as he went, "It was foolish of me to come here."

"You are wrong, Mr. Burrows." He heard the rustle of skirts as she got to her feet. "The only person who has emerged foolish from this affair is me. I believe you have been quite untouched."

The false sweetness had gone from her tone now, and because of what lingered underneath her words, Robert found himself pausing for a moment more before he opened the door. He turned and looked back at Miss Fairbank.

"I had no intention of making you feel foolish."

"But nevertheless, you have done so." Miss Fairbank paused, gazing at him for a moment before she continued, "When I met you, you know, Mr. Burrows, I saw you as you could be, not just as you were."

"As a baker, you mean?" Robert said at once. He saw her blink, as though surprised by his directness. "But I am a baker, and I might be worse." As he laid a hand on the doorhandle, he added, "It's an honest trade."

He went out, and she did not try to call him back again.

CHAPTER THIRTY-SIX

Hester had plenty of time to prepare herself for Robert's arrival in Manchester on the day before Christmas Eve, as for the whole week beforehand, his niece and nephew had not been able to talk of anything else. Their uncle Robert's yearly visit to Hope Street seemed, for them, to mark the true beginning of the festival. For Hester, it was a happy occasion, too, as to see Robert would always make her happy. But hers was not the kind of happiness that she saw shining in the faces of little Mary and Sam. It was a happiness that rejoiced in everything while expecting nothing. When she saw Robert step in the front door of Hope Street, shaking the snow from the collar of his coat and smiling that same old smile, prospects of air, light, and freedom opened up within her. The world seemed suddenly a brighter place, and even if he was not hers, that feeling was. Just as always, Hester felt happiest when she could see Robert like this, with herself standing separate from the picture.

Unfortunately, that window of time in which she could observe him unobserved was very short, for Hester was the patient who had made a miraculous recovery, the witness who had provided the evidence of Harold Fairbank's fraud, as well as being Mr. and Mrs. Locksmith's guest. All attention, it seemed, must be directed towards her. All conversation must have her as its object. Hester had never felt as uncomfortable as she did that evening. Everyone was so kind to her, while she sat there feeling stupid and strange. At dinner, trying to use the right knife and fork, in the drawing room at tea-time, trying to sew the lining on the purse that she was hoping to make as a present for Mrs. Locksmith, and all the while her clumsy fingers betraying her, she could have wished herself anywhere else if she had not felt that such a wish would be ingratitude to those who had helped her.

Robert was the kindest of everyone, his blue eyes continually seeking Hester out every time he made a remark or asked a question, even if neither remark nor question had been directed to her. She could tell by this that he wanted her to know that the old friendship was still there, waiting to be revived, that if she could only return his glance with that same happy confidence in her eyes, all would be just as it used to be. It was impossible for Hester to do this, of course, but she did have something to speak to

Robert about, and she preferred to do it sooner rather than later. So when a quiet moment came, after Mrs. Locksmith had taken the children up to bed and Mr. Locksmith had taken out a book, Hester put down her sewing and got up.

Moving in these stiff skirts, she still found, was a bit of a battle, though at least by now she had got one of Mr. Locksmith's old waistcoats to wear over her bodice, which made her feel a little bit more like herself. But the thing about wearing so much noisy fabric was that there was no way to take a person by surprise. Robert had already turned to greet her when she was only halfway to the bookshelf, and then she had to move the rest of the way with his eyes on her, feeling as though her arms were hanging very conspicuously by her sides.

"You've been quiet," he observed as she came to a halt beside him. "Are you tired?"

"Yes, that is, no, Robert. I mean Mr. Burrows."

"Please don't call me Mr. Burrows! I feel I'm about to break out in a sweat just from hearing it. It makes me imagine I've done something wrong."

"I'm the one who's done wrong," said Hester, and the smile that had been twitching at Robert's lips retreated. She went on, lowering her voice with a backwards glance at Mr. Locksmith, "I should have told you before agreeing to see that reporter. At the time I did it to help Mr. Locksmith, and because it was the right thing to do. I didn't think of how it might make things uncomfortable for Miss Fairbank."

Robert replaced the book that he had been looking at on the shelf, and he seemed to take his time adjusting its position before he responded, "I fear that it has made things uncomfortable for her. In fact, I know it for a fact, as I went to see her recently."

"I'm sure she didn't know what her father was really doing," Hester said quickly. Robert looked back down at her, consideringly.

"No, I don't think she did. But, Hester, you don't need to trouble yourself about such matters."

"I know it's not my place to interfere.–"

"I didn't mean to say that it wasn't your place."

"But I hope you will tell her that it was my fault," Hester finished, earnestly.

Robert was silent for a moment. He seemed to be thinking hard. "Even if I thought that was true, I don't think I'd have an opportunity to tell her such a thing. You see, I'm not likely to see her again."

"Oh," said Hester, blinking. She could feel his eyes on her as she looked around the room, as though she might find the right words in the fire that was blazing in the hearth or in the gently quivering needles of the Christmas tree. Things were worse, then, much worse than she had thought. It was all over between him and Miss Fairbank, but he had never complained, and, knowing Robert, she could not imagine that any resentment had lain behind his smiles and kind words to her that evening. It seemed that he really didn't blame her. At length, she managed to say, "I am very sorry to hear it."

In the silence that followed her words, Hester quickly excused herself to the two gentlemen and retired to bed, taking the half-finished purse with her.

CHAPTER THIRTY-SEVEN

Christmas Eve dawned wet and grey, with the morning's downpour chasing away all traces of snow from the street. Mary and Sam were disappointed by this, but when the weather cleared up in the afternoon, they came straight to Robert, eagerly anticipating their traditional walk around Oldham Street to look at other people's Christmas trees. In truth, this walk was really only ever an excuse to get the children out from under Lesley's feet, as she was always busy helping the cook prepare the stuffing and the goose for the next day. This year, Robert had no particular inclination for it, especially since he had been hoping to get Hester alone to properly explain to her the situation with Miss Fairbank. He had the feeling that something had been misunderstood in their conversation of last night. Judging by the anxious, sorrowful glances Hester had been casting him since breakfast, she seemed to think that he was nursing a broken heart. He wanted to make her see that it was not so bad as all that. Was he angry whenever he thought back on that last conversation with Simona Fairbank? Of course he was. And did he still think of her as the finest, most elegant young lady he had ever seen? Of course he did.

But Robert knew, even if he did not know much else these days, that there was a difference between a broken heart and wounded pride, and since he had last spoken to Miss Fairbank, he had been feeling more of the latter than anything else. Even though he had the last word, he kept thinking of cleverer things that he could have said and of ways that he could have steered the conversation so as to make himself appear to greater advantage. Above all, he hated feeling that he had emerged as the villain in the whole affair, when Miss Fairbank was the one who had never given an inch, who had used all her lady's graces and feminine tricks to make him believe that their brief courtship had been a matter of indifference to her, and then, at the last moment, had turned around and accused him of toying with her! Robert felt tired just thinking about it.

Hester had retreated to her room earlier that afternoon and had made no appearances since then, but Robert went all the same now to knock at her door and see if she wanted to join him, Mary, and Sam on the walk. There was a moment's pause after he had issued the invitation, and then Hester's voice sounded through the door. "Thank you for asking me, but I don't think I can."

There was an odd quality to her voice which made Robert frown. "Is everything all right?" He had his hand on the doorhandle, poised to turn it, but she called back at once,

"Yes, fine, perfectly fine! Thank you."

Raising his eyebrows, Robert went downstairs to get Mary and Sam ready, figuring that the mystery would be solved soon enough. They had gone a little way down the street when the sound of running footsteps came after them. Turning, Robert saw Hester, bare-headed and still forcing her arms into the sleeves of her coat, her cheeks flushed and her eyes bright with some emotion that he could not place. "You shouldn't run," he scolded her as she came level with them. "And where's your bonnet? Here." He scrabbled on his head and took off his cap, fixing it on Hester's dark head instead. Gruffly, he said, "So I take it you're coming with us after all, then?"

"Aye," said Hester, still breathless. "I wanted some fresh air."

"Well, come along. And take my arm if you start to feel weak."

"Uncle Rob is very bossy," Mary said in a carrying whisper to Hester, which Robert pretended not to hear.

They peered into the windows of houses that they passed on Oldham Street and argued with one another about which one had the best tree. Sometimes they would linger too long, and disgruntled faces would appear at the windows to block out their view of the decorations, at which point they would have to hurry on. Hester eventually did end up taking Robert's arm, though she held it so loosely that he couldn't imagine it was giving her much support at all. The presence of the children seemed to make her happier and lighter than he had seen her for a long time. He cast her sidelong glances from time to time, as she was pointing or marvelling at something, and the sight of her smile gave him a quiet kind of satisfaction.

When they had reached the end of the street, Robert murmured to Hester that it was still too early for them to return. She understood right away and let go of his arm as she called the children to her. Under her suggestion, a game of 'I spy' was soon underway, and as they made their slow way back up Oldham Road, passing the houses they had already seen, there were still lots of new things to be spied. Hester walked a little ahead of Robert, and he kept an eye on her the whole time, watching for the slightest suggestion of fatigue in her walk or posture. At one moment, when she slipped on an icy patch, he had his arm around her shoulders before he knew what he was doing, and she actually leaned back into his chest for a moment with an expression as though this was all perfectly natural to her. Robert, as surprised by her reaction as by his own, gazed down into her face, and it was only the eager voices of the children in their game that broke them apart.

He had forgotten completely about Hester's odd behaviour before their walk until the next day. After they had come back from church, it was time to exchange presents, and Mary and Sam exclaimed in delight when they saw that two new presents had been put aside for them, evidently right before they had left for church, for there was no way that they could have missed them in their morning's delighted perusal of the pile under the tree.

"Who are they from?" said Lesley, though she was smiling as though she already knew the answer.

The children turned over the parcels to find the label. Sam was the first to discover the mystery, and he exclaimed triumphantly, "Auntie Hester!"

"They're just small," Hester said hastily as everyone looked to her. "Very small. I just wanted to do something."

Sam was already ripping open the wrapping paper on his present, and a moment later he gave a whoop and held up a spinning top for everyone's inspection. It was made of wood, and when he set it on the table in the drawing room, it spun for three minutes. They all watched, Cecil and Lesley making an admiring remark every now and then, but Robert, who had been silent up until now, picked up the spinning top once it had fallen and looked at Hester. "Was this what you were doing yesterday in your room, when I came up to ask you to come walking with us?"

She nodded, looking abashed. "It didn't take very long. I just put together a wooden wheel and a dowel, but I was worried you, Mary, or Sam might come in and then the surprise would have been spoiled."

Everyone's attention was then turned to Mary, who had finally managed to rip her wrapping paper to reveal a skipping rope with gleaming wooden handles. "You made this too?" said Robert.

"Aye," said Hester, with a glance towards Cecil and Lesley, who were both smiling, "though I needed some help with the supplies."

Mary announced that she was going outside to try the rope out, and Lesley followed her to the garden, calling as she went, "Remember, dear, the ground will be wet from the rain!"

"I'm sorry," said Hester to Cecil and Robert. "I couldn't think of what to get you. I tried to make a purse for Mrs. Locksmith, but the lining got all snarled up."

"Not as good with your needle as you are with a hammer?" Robert said, grinning, and he got an uncertain smile in response.

"Really, Hester, you shouldn't worry," said Cecil. "You've done more than enough." Nudging his brother-in-law, "And, besides, Robert forgot me this year, too."

"I beg your pardon? What do you call that pair of cufflinks, then?"

241

"I call them a sorry excuse for a present."

They were then called out to help Lesley with Mary, who had already slipped and fallen on her first try of the rope but was unharmed and perfectly content once she'd relieved her feelings with a good cry.

Dinner was nothing like the stilted affair of the night before, uncertain faces in flickering candlelight. It was still light outside, for they always ate Christmas dinner in the late afternoon, and everyone was laughing and talking, even Hester, who gifted them with a detailed description of the Christmas fare at Brownlow Hill. "We were lucky if we got rabbit," she said, taking a sip of her wine. She gestured to the roasted goose and crisp potatoes, the young carrots, and cucumbers in white sauce. "Nothing like this. But they always told us to be thankful."

"'Be thankful,'" said Lesley with a laugh. "Oh, yes, we heard plenty of that growing up, too, didn't we, Rob?"

"It never stopped. We had to be thankful even for things we didn't have, in case we should have them one day."

"Well, we didn't do too badly in the end, I suppose," Lesley said, still smiling, gesturing to the table. Across from her, Cecil was silent. A shadow had fallen over his face.

"No," Robert agreed, with a glance at his brother-in-law, and they quickly changed the subject. Hester took another sip of her wine.

It was later, after the dishes had been cleared and stacked in the scullery, after the candles and the oil-lamp in the drawing room had been lit, that Robert went to look for Hester. He had seen the flush in her cheeks after the wine at dinner, and he had a good idea of where she might have gone to. Sure enough, she was standing out in the back garden, fanning herself. Her dark head was bare, short, uneven waves falling to her chin, and the hem of Lesley's old red dress was trailing on the ground.

"You know night air is deadly," said Robert as he approached her, "but it's all right, I won't tell the others."

Hester turned towards him, looking momentarily startled before she sighed. "I know I shouldn't be out in the cold, but I had to, you know." She gestured to herself. "I'm not used to being laced up like this." Then, catching something in Robert's expression, her eyes widened. "Oh, I shouldn't have said that, should I? It's not proper, talking about corsets and things."

"No," said Robert, laughing. "But you've said it now, and it's out in the open."

Hester smiled, but already she seemed to be thinking of something else. "Dinner was nice," she said, looking at him. "Very nice. You have a happy family."

"It wasn't always like that," Robert said quietly, looking down.

"But you're lucky, you know."

"I know," he said, after a moment. Then, taking a small brown parcel from under his arm, he held it out to Hester. "Here."

"But I didn't get you…"

"It's not really a Christmas present. I'm just returning something that was already yours. Come over where you can see it." Robert took hold of Hester's elbow and steered her towards the illuminated patch of garden outside the kitchen window.

She unwrapped the paper with trembling fingers and held up the book. *The Little Mermaid*! Oh!" A note had fallen out of the pages, and she caught it before it hit the ground. "It's from Mr. Moss, wishing me a happy Christmas."

"After we found you that day," Robert said, "you still had the book on you. It was wet, almost soaked through, and we barely managed to prise it from your fingers. I brought it home to Mr. Moss and he dried out the pages in his cellar. He told me that if you and I don't start taking better care of our books, he's going to ban us from the stand."

Hester laughed with her hand over her mouth. It was difficult to tell in the dim light, but Robert thought he saw tears in her eyes. "I thought I'd lost it," she said, holding up the book cover close to her face.

"I should have told you, maybe. But, I suppose, I wanted to fix it first, and see that it was readable. And I wanted to read it myself."

"Did you?" Hester slowly lowered the book to her side, watching him carefully.

"Aye. One night when I was waiting for the dough to rise. I tried to sleep but couldn't. I came down and took it out, and I read it all through without moving from my chair." Robert shook his head. Hester had gone absolutely still. "I must say, I didn't like that ending."

"It's sad," she said softly.

"It's not just sad, it's –" Robert gritted his teeth. "It made me angry. To think that after everything the little mermaid does for that prince, saving his life, giving up her voice and all her friends, her family and her life in the sea, after everything she does, he falls in love with another woman?"

"He didn't know," said Hester.

"He should have known. She was always there."

"But she couldn't tell him. She didn't have her voice. And anyway, she was happy to be by his side as his friend. She was happy if he was happy."

"No. You know what she should have done at the end of the story? She should have stabbed the prince and his new wife just like the sea-witch told her to do and won back her freedom and her old life."

"But she couldn't have!" Hester gave an incredulous laugh as she looked at him. "She loved him! Maybe you should read it again. I don't think you understood the story."

"No, I understood it," Robert said, in a low voice, and the smile faded from Hester's face. "And I want to say that I'm sorry."

"You don't have to be." She had started to back away from him. "You did nothing to apologise for."

"I was careless. I was thoughtless. I sent you to carry messages to Miss Fairbank and it never occurred to me that you might…"

"Why should it?" Hester exclaimed. "We were friends! And I was happy to be your friend." At the sound of voices from within, she glanced towards the kitchen window and then towards the door. "I'd better go back in."

"Wait just a minute more," Robert said. "Please. Hester." She looked back at him. "How could you have done it? How could you have done all those things for me and never said a word? I was in love with Miss Fairbank for a month and it almost killed me. How long have you…"

"Since the start," Hester told him, matter-of-factly. "Since I met you."

Robert breathed out slowly. "And all that time. Hester, you didn't have to be a hero, you know. You might have said something. I understand why you didn't at the start, but when everything happened with Miss Fairbank, well, you might have made things easier on yourself."

"I wasn't trying to be a hero." Her voice was almost a whisper now. "I just didn't want to be greedy."

This threw Robert. "Greedy? What do you…"

But Hester was backing away again. "Thank you for the book," she said, before slipping back into the house.

CHAPTER THIRTY-EIGHT

W ith the New Year came a change in the mood at the house on Hope Street. It had not snowed in Manchester since the day before Christmas Eve, and such weather did not seem likely to come again. Sam and Mary started complaining about having to go back to school, and Mr. and Mrs. Locksmith resumed their hushed conferences that no one could help overhearing. It was very plain what was on their minds, though they did not share their burdens with either Robert or Hester. More mills and warehouses had closed in Manchester during the past month besides Cecil's own, and at all hours of the day, outside those places in town that were still open, men, women and children could be seen waiting in long lines, clutching their shawls and caps as the driving rain soaked them through.

The decorations were taken down on the day of the Epiphany, much to the children's regret, and such feelings were compounded by their uncle's imminent departure. Hester knew about it, and, in a way, looked forward to it. Though she knew now that Robert was not engaged, that knowledge almost made things worse. It fairly divided her, most of the time, between hope and fear, hope for the impossible, and fear of the inevitable. Miss Fairbank, for all the pain that her existence had given Hester, had been a known quantity. But what of the next young lady who would walk into Robert's shop and cause that light to come into his eyes? Hester might not see it happen this time, and she might have to hear about it secondhand, which seemed like it would be worse. For there was no question that she would be going back to Liverpool, to her home. And to separate her life there from Robert, though she had thought of doing it once, was similarly out of the question.

A knock came on Hester's door as she was writing a letter to Mr. Moss. Last week she had written to thank him for what he had done with her book, and they had started up a strange kind of correspondence. His letters were always brief and wandered from subject to subject, each change seemingly unprompted, before winding up with some question. In his last one he had asked her when she was coming back to Liverpool. Hester smiled as she wrote down her last sentence, and called out, "Come in!"

Robert stepped in, and was silent for a moment, so that Hester turned around and got up from her chair. "What is it?"

"You're not packed?" he asked, looking around as though he expected to see a suitcase hiding in the corner of the room. He was wearing his overcoat and the blue scarf that his sister had gotten him for Christmas.

Rather than telling him that she would not have had very much to pack in the first place, Hester said, "No, I'm not going. Not yet, anyway. I thought Mrs. Locksmith would have mentioned it to you."

"You can call her Lesley, you know. She keeps saying it. I thought you were going with me?" That familiar, faint frown was creasing Robert's forehead now.

"No," said Hester again, "I thought I'd go with Mr. Locksmith. He's travelling to Liverpool next week to meet with a reporter about the Fairbank case, so it's convenient for him if we go together."

"It would be just as convenient if you travelled with me," said Robert, and Hester had to look away. A heavy silence followed which she had no intention of breaking. Finally he said, with some of his former lightness,

"Very well. But you are still coming back?"

Hester nodded, still without looking at him.

"Good," said Robert, and she could hear the smile in his voice. "Then we can say goodbye here, if you prefer."

Hester made herself look at him and took a halting step forward. He closed the rest of the distance between them and shook her hand. And it would have been all right if that was all it was, a handshake between two acquaintances meeting on the street, but Robert held her hand for rather longer than necessary, and looked into her eyes, so that, just for a moment, that impossible hope didn't seem so impossible after all.

"Happy New Year," he said. "Until we meet again."

She wished him a safe journey, and when he was gone, sank back down into her chair, one part disappointed and three parts relieved.

CHAPTER THIRTY-NINE

Lesley Locksmith was very apologetic to Hester when her husband's meeting with the reporter was cancelled, and she offered to travel with her to Liverpool in his stead, but Hester insisted that she would be all right on her own.

"Really, ma'am, I'm feeling stronger every day, and it's only a short journey." She remembered how frighteningly fast it had felt on the way over here. Had that only been in October?

"I suppose it's no use telling you again to call me Lesley, since you never seem to listen. I'll walk you to the station, in any case. Cecil has the carriage, I'm afraid, so we'd better bring an umbrella. Children, come say goodbye to Miss Grace."

Mary and Sam came running up the hall, and Hester, bending, got a hug and a kiss from each. She was carrying a small carpet bag which Mrs. Locksmith had stuffed full of old clothes, telling Hester that she refused to let her leave the house without them. Since practically everything Hester was wearing now had used to belong to Mrs. Locksmith, she supposed it didn't make much of a difference if she brought a few more things with her. But she was looking forward to getting back to Liverpool and getting her own clothes. *With what money?* a voice in her head prompted, and Hester shook it away. That was a problem for tomorrow. Once, she had been used to living her life like this, taking each day as it came and being content if she survived each night. She was sure that she could go back to it, though it might take some getting used to after the last month and a half.

"The children are going to miss you," Mrs. Locksmith said as they set off for the station. There was a fog down and a light drizzle over their heads. When they reached the end of the street, Mrs. Locksmith put up her umbrella and joined her arm with Hester's so that they could crowd beneath it. "We're all going to miss you, in fact."

"After all the trouble I caused?"

"You were no trouble," Mrs. Locksmith said at once, "at least, not in that way." She paused. "Though you did give Robert quite a scare. When he found out that you were in Manchester, alone, and that the boy you'd gone to find wasn't even in the same city…"

"It was stupid," said Hester, "but I felt bad about Fred. I thought I could have done more. But he was always out for his own, just like all those other kids."

"In those two weeks, when we were searching for you," Mrs. Locksmith went on, "Robert was like a man possessed. I don't think I've ever seen him like that, not even when our little brother died, and he nearly went mad back then. Robert loves with his whole heart, you know. Not like some people who corner off a part of it and leave the rest boxed up."

"I know," said Hester quietly. "He's good to his friends. He's good to everyone."

"That wasn't what I..." Then Mrs. Locksmith seemed to stop herself. "Anyway. Are you enough under the shelter? Your head isn't getting wet?"

Hester reassured her as to that point, and they walked on in silence for a few minutes until Hester ventured a question.

"I hope you don't mind me asking, but you, Mr. Locksmith, and the children, are you going to be all right?"

Mrs. Locksmith sighed. "Yes, well, I hope so. We will have to sell the house and perhaps we won't be able to keep servants anymore. But that must seem quite trivial to you."

"It doesn't," said Hester, surprised. "Everyone has their burdens."

"But, perhaps some more than others." Hester sensed Mrs. Locksmith looking at her. "What are you going to do, when you go back to Liverpool?"

"What I've always done, I reckon," Hester replied, and then, in firmer tones, "And I wouldn't want it any other way." Glancing sidelong at her companion, she said, "You see, ma'am, what I can't stand is being locked up somewhere, at someone's beck and call, sleeping, eating, and working all in the same place and never seeing the sun."

"I think most people couldn't stand that," said Mrs. Locksmith quietly. "And yet so many have to."

They had passed one of the long lines of unemployed men and women, outside Carter's mill on Portland Street. Hester looked back and bit her lip. "I know it might look strange to you," she told Mrs. Locksmith as she faced forward again. "My way of life. But it's fixed so I can see the sun, breathe the air, walk the streets as I like and they're my own. In Liverpool, I mean, not here."

"Of course. It's home."

"It's more than home. It's me, all of me."

They walked for a few minutes in silence. The station loomed up before them sooner than Hester had been expecting, and there was a queue outside there, too, waiting for the ticket office. Hester thought again of her manner of arrival here, of the disorienting journey and the crowded platform, the long walk through dark, unfamiliar streets. It seemed only right, too, that she should leave Manchester just as she had come to it, wrapped in one of its thick blue fogs.

"You don't have to wait," she told Mrs. Locksmith, but of course Mrs. Locksmith would not hear of doing anything else, and after they had queued for half an hour and gotten Hester's ticket, she walked with her into the station. When they got to the platform, the steam from the train engines had combined with the fog to make it nearly impossible to see anything. All around them, they heard the quick passage of invisible feet and disembodied voices calling out to one another. More than once, as they walked down alongside the train towards the third-class carriage, an elbow or shoulder would come out of seemingly nowhere to knock into them, always accompanied by a hasty apology before whatever passenger it belonged to had moved on.

"We still have a few minutes," said Mrs. Locksmith, raising her voice over the din. "I'll come and sit with you till they blow the whistle."

"You don't have to." Hester started, but then she felt the firm pressure of Mrs. Locksmith's hand, taking the carpet bag from her grip and guiding her onto the train.

This carriage was actually roofed, as opposed to the one that Hester had travelled in on her way here, which meant it was not quite as cold as that one had been, and it was still empty enough that they had their pick of the seats. Mrs. Locksmith let Hester choose, and then she sat in the seat opposite her, placing the carpet bag on the floor between them.

"It was so loud out there," she said, shaking her head. "Here we can talk. Hester, there's something I want to say to you."

Hester could only watch in trepidation as Mrs. Locksmith drew from her pocket an envelope. "There's something I've been told to say to you, in fact," the older woman went on. "I've been very strictly instructed, by Robert. Before he left last week, he gave me this to give to you. And he told me to tell you... I can't make head nor tail of this, but he said to tell you that he still thinks the sea-witch was right."

Hester smiled before she could help herself. Mrs. Locksmith raised her eyebrows. "So that does mean something to you, then. I'm glad. I was half afraid Robert was making some kind of joke." She hesitated for a moment more, and then held out the envelope to Hester. "But only half afraid because he was very serious about the rest of it. He wanted me to do things in the right way. He wanted me to give you time after he left, to wait before giving you this. As you see, I've waited until the last possible minute. But I had my own reasons for doing that."

Hester was holding the envelope now, so loosely that it was in danger of falling out of her hand.

"I think I can guess what is in that letter," Mrs. Locksmith went on. Hester started to shake her head. "And if my guess is right, then it's good news. But I must tell you, Hester, it was hard for me to help Robert in this way; harder than you might expect and perhaps harder than he could have imagined. You see, I know how you feel. You're shaking your head again, but I'm telling you it's true. Cecil might have loved me from the first, but there were always other claims on him. His aunt wanted him to marry well. He wanted to rise high. I couldn't be more than I was, and there were times when I wondered if I would be enough. I think there were times when he wondered that, too." Looking out the window at the steam-shrouded platform, Mrs. Locksmith's eyes were far away. "And I remember, Hester, when I was around your age, standing in a station like this and feeling so terribly afraid, knowing that whatever I did next, or whatever he did next, would decide our fate."

Hester had clutched the envelope to her breast and closed her arms over it, because her hands were shaking so hard that she couldn't maintain any kind of grip.

"I don't think that men understand the kind of fear that we can feel, when we love. I don't think they will ever understand it. Your brother, Cecil, any of them. No matter how kind or good they might be, they just love in a different way." Up the platform, the whistle blew, and

Mrs. Locksmith straightened up, her gaze returning to Hester. "But that's enough of that. Hester, my dear, I'll leave you now. I hope, with all my heart, that you don't need to be afraid of whatever is in that letter. But just know, whatever happens, that you will always have friends in us."

Lesley Locksmith smiled at Hester, in parting. Her smile was not like her brother's. It had none of the same startling openness as his, for it did not transform her face. There was something tired in it. Looking at Mrs. Locksmith's smile, Hester could feel the truth of her words. She knew, without a doubt, that this woman had known fear. Not just any fear, either, but the kind of fear in which Hester had lived ever since she had first clapped eyes on Robert four years before. It was the kind of fear that Hester had sometimes thought might kill her, and that she knew she could not possibly live without.

CHAPTER FORTY

ester read Robert's letter as the train was coming out of Manchester. Her eyes scanned the words quickly, and she neither saw nor heard anything of what was going on around her. When she had read it once over, she read it through again. Then she read it a third time. She thought, with a wonderful kind of panic, that she might be reading such a letter for the rest of her life.

'Dear Hester,' the letter began. 'I've conscripted Lesley as our go-between, and I hope she has done as I asked and waited a little while before giving this letter to you. I don't want you to think that this is some mad impulse of mine. In fact it's something I have been thinking about for a long time, though I don't really know when it started, maybe when you were ill and we thought we might lose you, or maybe further back.

'You said, when we spoke in the garden on Christmas night, that you've been silent about your feelings, all that time that we knew each other, because you didn't want to be "greedy". I couldn't understand what you meant then, but over the last week I've thought about it, and it has become a bit clearer to me. And there are two things that I want to say. The first, Hester, is that I don't think there was ever a danger of you being greedy. You never ask anything of anyone. In fact, I think that you ask too little. Which leads me to my second point. If you could ask for something now, in this moment, for anything in this world, what would it be? Would it be me?

'I hope that your answer to that is "yes". I don't presume, of course, but I hope. Because when you come back to Liverpool, I'd like you to live with me again. We'd do things properly this time, don't worry. We'd live together as man and wife. I don't just ask you this because I know you'd keep the clocks running in good time, or because I've got so used to having you around that these last few months have been strange and lonely. I ask you this because I never want to be parted from you again. You've been many things to me these past few years, Hester, a friend, a confidante, a go-between, and now I ask you to be my wife.

'I won't run on anymore. Think it over. Take as much time as you need, only, if you please, have some compassion for a baker in Liverpool who will be anxiously waiting to learn his fate, and who is, and always will be,

Yours, Robert.'

.   .   .

As Hester put down the letter upon her third reread, she happened to look out the window and saw that they were not yet out of sight of the Manchester skyline. The first feelings of shock at this discovery, that, though an eternity seemed to have passed for her, for everyone else on the train it had only been a few minutes, soon gave way to those of wonder, as she saw the thick blue fog around the city pierced through its core by a ray of golden sunlight.

CHAPTER FORTY-ONE

Hester had dreamed, what felt like a long time ago, of running down Cobbler's Lane at nightfall to find Robert waiting for her at the back door of the bakery. Now it was not quite nightfall, but rather a grey January dusk, and Robert was not waiting for her at the back door. But that back door was unlocked, and Hester stepped in, looking around at the back room, whose table had been laid with one setting for supper. She saw then that the kitchen door stood half-open, and went to it with a thumping heart, slipping in through the gap. When she saw Robert, the oven door was standing between them, obscuring his face. He seemed to take forever rearranging the trays before he finally closed it with a clang, saw her, and stared.

Other parts of Hester's long-ago dream soon came true. She was in Robert's arms, her face buried in his shoulder as she shook with tears and laughter. For a long time, he just held her tightly to him. When, at length, he drew back, it was only to untie his apron and lead her by hand into the back room, where he laid another setting for her at the table and sat her down just as he had done so many times before. But when they were seated across from each other, butter, bread, honey, and a pot of tea between them, all of which looked and smelled wonderful and none of which Hester could appreciate as she should have, Robert looked at her and seemed to come to some decision. He rose from his chair, the legs scraping back across the floor, and walked around to her chair, where he stopped. Since he seemed to be waiting for something, Hester rose, on trembling legs, to meet him. He passed a hand over her forehead, down the line of her temple just as far as it met her jaw, and he kept it there as he leaned in and kissed her gently.

"I know I have a bit of catching up to do," Robert said sometime later, after they had eaten. He was sitting on the settee with Hester on his lap, and his arms looped around her waist. She had her ear to his shoulder, so that she could hear the vibrations of his voice. "I'm a bit behind. Really, you've been very patient with me."

"Everyone has their limits," Hester murmured. "A few months later and maybe I would have run out." Then she kissed Robert on the cheek to show him that she was joking. He laughed a bit, and then, in more serious tones,

"But you did run out. That is, you ran away. You must promise me never to do that again."

Hester kissed him again, this time on the lips, and this distracted him enough that he did not press her to give him an answer. She would not, and could not, give such a promise. It wasn't just that a little fear remained in her, and would always remain, that one day Robert would get tired of her and set his sights on someone new, and that her agony would begin again. It was that, though she might have her prince now, she was still a spirit of air. She belonged to the Mersey, in its cold grey stillness, and the winter sky with its hail, snow, and rain, and she belonged to the ragged children on Albert Dock. She was still one of them, running among them, hunting out whatever scraps of warmth and friendship were thrown their way. She belonged to Brownlow Hill, to its grim, hard face that frowned over the city. And she belonged to two poor, lost people who were likely dead, her parents whom she had never known and who had never known her, who had likely never expected her to come into the world. Hester Grace would never be Robert's alone, and maybe he knew that. Maybe he didn't. Over the years that followed their marriage, they would learn many things about each other and about the world around them. But since their souls were used to hardship, since he was always ready to smile and she was always ready to love, Robert Burrows and Hester Grace had a better chance at happiness than most.

CHAPTER FORTY-TWO

The war in America ended up lasting longer than anyone had expected, and when those four years were over, it seemed that things in Britain had changed forever. The cotton trade would never be the same. The jobs that had been lost could never be got back again, and the many families who had been touched by the cold hand of poverty could not simply turn back the clock. Some of the mills and warehouses in Manchester reopened, but a good number, including Cecil's own, remained closed forever.

Cecil and Lesley moved from Hope Street to a smaller house in Spinning Fields, which had no garden for Mary and Sam to run around in and where the air was worse than in many other parts of Manchester. For a time, they talked of moving to Liverpool, but then a new opportunity emerged from unexpected quarters. Byron

Davies, to whose daughter Cecil had once been engaged and whose business empire had crashed during the '50s, was seeking to invest in a new modification of the power loom which would reduce the number of weavers required in the manufacture of cotton. Davies, having been gratified by the article in the *Herald* that had at last exposed Fairbank as the fraud that he was, wanted Cecil to join him in this new investment. Although the opportunity seemed unlikely to yield results, especially since Davies, by now, had a history of making unwise investments, Cecil, against his wife's advice, hitched his wagon to Byron Davies's and invested what little he had. In the space of two years they were seeing returns, as this new, modified power loom came into use in more mills around Manchester. Though the house on Hope Street had long since been sold, Cecil and Lesley were able to move to more comfortable quarters on Oldham Street, and their children, now in their teens, were able once more to hold their heads up high among their peers. This was especially important for Mary, whom Lesley and Cecil hoped would make a good match one day.

Mr. Fairbank did not end up serving time for his fraud, but his business was soon affected by another scandal. A year after the damning article in the *Herald* had been published, one of Mr. Fairbank's most loyal workmen, a foreman in his offices by the name of John Farrell, was arrested for assault of a woman on Albert Dock, and with the arrest of that man soon followed more accusations from others, men and women, who had been menaced or attacked by him. Hester Burrows, reading of the arrest in the papers one day during hers and Robert's dinner hour, put a hand to the table as she sighed out her relief, for since that day with Farrell she had never returned to Albert Dock alone. She had never told Robert of the encounter, nor would she. There were some secrets that Hester Burrows would always keep close to herself, without ever understanding why.

Miss Simona Fairbank married her eligible match and moved to a large house on the outskirts of Liverpool. She never came to Robert's bakery again, although often she could be seen shopping on Lime Street with other ladies of status. Whenever she and Robert passed each other, it was always with a nod of the head, sometimes with a bow and a curtsy if they had the leisure for such a greeting. Since only Hester, a few servants, and Mr. Fairbank had known of their brief courtship, the affair was soon forgotten, for which fact Miss Fairbank, now Mrs. Forster, was exceedingly grateful. Even as others might forget, she would never forget the sting of being rejected by someone who was so much lower than her, and, for that matter, rejected for an urchin from Albert Dock! When Mrs. Forster heard of Robert and Hester's marriage, she was not particularly surprised, but she was furious. After Mr. Burrows had so vehemently denied that there existed anything between him and Hester beyond mere friendship, to go and marry that little 'friend' of his was, in Mrs. Forster's eyes, unassailable proof of his duplicity. Never again, she swore, would she allow herself to be put in such a humiliating position, and, accordingly, she always adopted a very chilly manner with her husband's workmen whenever she had the misfortune of having to deal with them. The men, thus snubbed, murmured to one another about the boss's wife 'fancying herself' a little and thought no more about it.

Lesley Locksmith, alienated for a time from Cecil after he had refused to take her advice about investing with Mr. Davies, began to return to her hometown more often. She was always welcome at the bakery, and she and Hester, whose friendship had been cemented in that short but vital conversation in Manchester station, never ran out of things to talk about. They found that, even though they were married to good men, there was no shortage of fear and uncertainty in their lives. Indeed, often it seemed that their lives without those good men had been so much simpler and easier. Hester, from time to time, found herself thinking with a little regret of the freedom that she had lost, though Lesley, if she had any such longings, kept them to herself.

When Cecil's risky investment ended up paying off, he and Lesley mended fences, and the latter's visits to Liverpool became less frequent. But in her place, another visitor soon arrived. Hester, who had for a few years had been informed by the surgeon that the thing she and

Robert longed for might not be possible, found that a new kind of joy was soon to enter her life. Seven years after they had married, Robert and Hester had a daughter, and that child opened her eyes to a world that was much more hopeful than the one into which her father and mother had been born. Growing up on Cobbler's Lane, little Katie Burrows was watched out for by all the neighbours, and at an early age, under Mr. Moss's guidance, she learned to love and care for books. Under her father's guidance, she learned patience and diligence, and that a happy confidence in the results of one's work could often supply any other lack thereof. From her mother, Hester, she learned the gift of hope and the art of dreaming, and such things were to serve her years later, for there would come dark times in happy, pretty Katie Burrows's life just as in any other.

Fred Small carried on living from day to day just as he always had, running with one gang for a time before moving on to another. He always seemed in some kind of trouble, but nothing would ever stick to him. Though he went by a new name now and had abandoned his rather conspicuous fine clothes by necessity, Hester would always call him Gentleman Fred, and he submitted to this with a good grace. He did, after all, have a soft spot for Hester, as much as he might have denied it to anyone who asked. And it was for this reason, and this reason alone, that he often came around to the bakery, and never because he was hungry, frightened, or maybe even a little lonely. He felt that Hester needed his friendship, and had decided, very generously, to grant such friendship to her wherever he could. Hester, for her part, never quite got over feeling guilty for those times that she had let Fred down and spent the rest of her days trying to make up for them. But she never left Fred alone in the bakery, for she knew that, though he was good deep down, he could only be trusted to be himself.

Robert Burrows found that, though married life was not the horror that he had once dreamed it to be, there were hardships that came with it which he would never have expected. He always worried about Hester, though he would never admit this to her, and at the back of his mind lay the fear that one day she would disappear, just as she had done once before, only that this time, he might not be able to find her in time. There were other little secrets that Robert kept close to his breast, just as Hester kept little secrets from him. For instance, he never told her that the name of their daughter, Katie, had been the name of a young, sick girl whom he had loved once upon a time, when he was just a boy growing up in Vauxhall. The girl had died, and others had forgotten her, but Robert never did.

But he loved his work, and he loved Hester, little Katie, and Liverpool, and most of the time, such love was enough, even if the price Robert paid for it was a weight of responsibility that never left his shoulders. He had seen, in his own childhood, what a bad father and husband could be, and strove never to be accused of the same. Little did Robert know just how far he was from that title, or with just how much adoration he was really regarded by his wife and daughter. One saw him always as her prince, and the other, more simply, as the best, wisest, and kindest man in the world. Robert, for his part, knew that Hester spoiled Katie a bit since she didn't know how else to love, and so he tried to be a bit harder on their daughter, to push her when she needed to be pushed and to prepare her for those hard knocks that would inevitably come. But with Hester, he was always gentle, because he knew that she had not known much gentleness in her life. The world around them, he hoped, was becoming a gentler place, but it might be years before they could see the effects of that slow change. In the meantime, Robert Burrows knew the power of a smile and an outstretched hand, in chasing away the darkness.

THANK YOU FOR CHOOSING A PUREREAD BOOK!

We hope you enjoyed the story, and as a way to thank you for choosing PureRead we'd like to send you this free book, and other fun reader rewards...

Click here for your free copy of Whitechapel Waif
PureRead.com/victorian

Thanks again for reading.

HAVE YOU READ?

THE DESPERATE CHRISTMAS ANGEL

Now that you have read 'The Orphan Girl and The Baker' *why not continue with another hope-filled Victorian Christmas Romance.*

Hester's story was one that crossed society lines in favour of love. A similar surprise awaits another young girl in a wonderful PureRead tale you'll adore called *The Desperate Christmas Angel.*

With Christmas fast approaching little does Eliza Thorn realise that her straightforward life of toil and danger is about to change irrevocably, when she comes across a stranger almost swallowed in icy waters...

Here for your enjoyment is the beginning of Eliza's story.

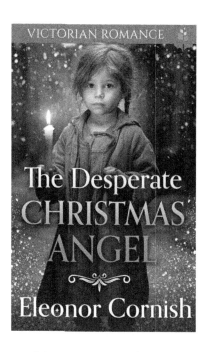

VICTORIAN ROMANCE

The Desperate
CHRISTMAS
ANGEL

Eleonor Cornish

There was something very satisfying about the crunch underfoot as Eliza trudged over the frost-covered ground. She took a strange delight in finding small, frozen puddles and deliberately pressing on them with her boot. She did not know why, but she found a thrill in watching the ice shatter into tiny shards, discovering not a drop of liquid water beneath. The hardened mud was equally fascinating to the young girl, and she looked out for boot prints she had made in the last days. Seeing these preserved marks in the ground scattered alongside trails of water birds and the occasional fox gave the winter-locked moors a certain timeless quality, a sense of the eternal in a world that was so often changeable and impermanent.

As she trudged haphazardly over the frozen mud banks, Eliza took time to admire the shadows about her, the ghostly suggestion of dead logs, half sunk trees leaning heavily in the peat, the occasional shrub eking out a solitary existence on the scattered islands of dry ground that rose above the waterline. The thick morning fog was a constant on the moorland. In summer, the veil of mist was lit up in a golden sheen, bathing Eliza's world in an almost heavenly glow. In winter, the grey mists were almost impenetrable, Eliza's eyes only able to see twenty or thirty feet in any direction. Walking alone among the indistinct shadows made her feel like she was moving through some waking dream state, everything insubstantial and ethereal except for her. Some would have found the shrouded isolation of the moors depressing, melancholic, but not Eliza. She found the barely navigable and ever-changing waterways exciting, calling to her sense of adventure and discovery as she charted her way through the unmapped fog.

An expert in judging the ground beneath her, Eliza made her way across the boggy ground without once slipping into the ice filmed water or straying onto a damp patch of mud that had not yet frozen over. Eliza prided herself on how well she moved across the quagmire, claiming often that she was lighter than air to her younger brother who lacked the balance and shrewd eye to make it across the bogs.

Coming to a suitable place to begin her work, Eliza shrugged off the large satchel she carried, laying it down on the firm, frozen grasses where she stood. Then, bending down, she tested the mud around her. The slight sheen on the surface suggested the ground was still damp and she nodded approvingly as her finger sank easily into the cold muck. She withdrew her hand and wiped the dirt off on a rag she had stuffed away in her bag. Taking off her coat and laying it down by her pack, Eliza shuddered momentarily from the cold that nipped at her. She rubbed her arms and blew out a sigh, watching as the steam carried from her lips onto the frostbitten air. The cold was something she would simply have to endure for a time, and the small girl tried to reassure herself that her coat would feel all the warmer when she put it on again.

Rolling up the sleeves of her dress, Eliza once again returned to her knees, leaning as far over the damp mud as she dared without risking falling in. She bunched up her face, lips disappearing altogether as she drove her arms deep into the mud.

The liquid ooze was thick and cold. Eliza did not much care for it in any season, but winter was by far the most testing time for her. She drove her arms in up to the elbows then became still as she let herself adjust to the cold bite of the muck and stagnant water pooled around her. To help with the process, she looked up, staring into the fog and enjoying, once again, the ethereal shadows that surrounded her on all sides. She could see the curtain-like branches of an old willow somewhere ahead, the tree looking like a long-necked woman with her hair cascading down into the water. Elsewhere, a wood pigeon could be heard calling out through the gloom. Narrowing her eyes and focusing a little harder still, Eliza was sure she could see the distinctive spindle legs and noble frame of a heron trudging slowly through the mud, questing through the mire for some fish or perhaps a hibernating frog to enjoy for its breakfast.

At last, the chill bite of the muddy water subsided, and Eliza felt able to begin her work. Pulling her arms out of the water, she grabbed a jar from her satchel and then plunged it deep into the water. This time, she pushed her arms even further into the muck, trying to reach the very bottom. She scooped the thickest mud into the jar and then hauled her arms out. It was hard going. The thick mud held her fast, a horrible wet sound echoing across the wetlands as she fought the suction. At last, though, she pulled herself free and was able to pour the mud out onto the bank beside her. She spread the muck thin over the frosted grass, smiling with relief as she immediately spotted three black, blob-like entities that lay dormant and still among the ooze.

Leeches.

Opening up a second jar, Eliza deposited the three leeches inside, leaving the lid open. The tiny parasites inside did not move at all, each frozen in winter hibernation, which was exactly how Eliza liked them.

Leech picking was no job for the faint of heart. No matter the season, there was always some element of the job to be reviled and hated. In winter, it was the cold and chill of working in the icy waters that got to Eliza. However, at least in those months, the Leeches were nothing more than jewelled blobs she had to dig out of the mud where they slept. In summer, leeching was a good deal easier and a good deal more painful at once. In the warmer months, when the foul parasites were active in the waters, Eliza had to use her own body as bait to catch the little bloodsuckers. She would wade out into the shallow waters and simply wait for the leeches to become attracted to her. They would latch onto her flesh with their cruel jaws, their body's pulsating and fattening as they sucked her blood. She would pull each one off her body and deposit them in a jar just as she was doing now, but the act of pulling the lock-jawed creatures from her flesh was always painful. Even after years at the work, Eliza still felt a sharp sting every time one of the bloodsuckers attached themselves to her and every time she pried them off her.

Shuddering as a stiff breeze whipped through the willows and across her back, Eliza tried to remember the pains of hunting for leeches in the summer, reassuring herself that she was better off frozen and bite-free than warm and riddled with marks all down her legs.

The morning's work was favourable for Eliza. As the sun rose and the mists that surrounded the waters eased, she felt quite confident she would be finished with her grim duty before afternoon. Mr Barrows, the village doctor, would be impressed with her time and the number of leeches she had collected over the morning—three jars full. Buoyed by her success, Eliza allowed herself a moment of repose, pulling her arms out of the mud and resting on the banks for a few minutes. Common sense told her she would be better off finishing her work. The sooner she topped off her last jar with leeches for the doctor, the sooner she could be home and warming by the fire. Still, Eliza wanted the break, and she enjoyed the views of the still, quiet moorland that stretched out before her. At least, the moors were almost still.

Somewhere farther away in the thinning mists, Eliza spied a figure moving through the mud. She could not make out any details, just a shadow, arms spread wide and stance constantly shifting. No doubt, whoever the explorer of the bogs was, they were unused to moving over the shifting mud. The heron that had spent the morning prowling the waters took to the air, angered by the interruption the blustering interloper was causing. Eliza frowned, watching the shadow closer as it seemed to struggle to find its way. She knew almost all the fishermen, fellow leech collectors and ramblers who wandered the fenlands, and none of them would have so hard a time navigating the mud. She could only assume, whoever was ahead of her was new to the task and she could not help but worry.

Twice in quick succession, the shadow seemed to dip, a poorly placed foot sinking into the mud and threatening to send the shadow falling into the mire. Each time, the shadow righted itself, but Eliza's fears were growing moment by moment. There were not many accidents or deaths recorded out on the fens, but they were not unheard of either. Almost always they involved some drunkard or a bold fool who had ventured out across the swamp without fully appreciating the dangers and challenges the wetlands posed.

Eliza's body was tense, and she knew she could not return to her work while some idiot was blustering about and at risk of harming themselves. Forgetting the possibility of an early finish and the fire of home, Eliza resolved to leave her pack and jars and go to the stranger's aid. However, just as she stood and looked to ensure her things were secure, a cry caused her to look up with fearful eyes. The shadow was gone, disappeared beneath the waters.

Young Edward Stanford had stormed off onto the fens without much preparation or forethought. Impetuous by nature, governed by his heart rather than his head, he could have done little less when his elder brother had dared him to venture out across the wetlands and bring back a toad as proof of his success.

Edward was in a long and protracted war with his brother —at least he saw it that way. Martin was always crowing about his rank and seniority as the elder brother, always eager to remind his little brother how his fortunes would rise and fall on his say so. In Martin's mind, Edward was little more than a glorified servant of the household, someone to boss about and order as he saw fit. If Edward objected, Martin would remind his little brother of his place and recite again all he could do in adulthood to make his life a misery.

Of course, Edward did not stand easily for his brother's jibes and threats. Though young, he was not to be intimidated by those older or bigger than him. It had led to more than a few tousles between the lads, Edward inevitably leaving the fight with a bruise or black eye. When their mother had intervened and finally warned Martin to watch his manners around his younger brother, Martin had found a new way to keep his irksome pest of a sibling at bay…. dares.

Whenever Martin did not wish to be bothered by Edward or felt a need to punish his younger brother for some misdeed or other, Martin would invent some new dare and 'test of courage' for Edward to overcome to prove himself a man. In the last six months, he had his little brother climbing the tallest tree on the estate and stranding himself in its upper boughs, spending the night in the hayloft of the stables and bringing their mother into a frightened panic when it seemed her youngest had run away from home, and even had Edward steal their father's gold-plated pen from his office. That last hiding had earned Edward a severe rap across the knuckles and Mr Stanford had all but denied his existence for a good fortnight afterward.

Now, Edward had been convinced to embark on another quest to prove himself: to venture out into the frozen, winter-locked waters of the mudflats and find a hibernating toad. Once again, Edward had fallen for his brother's mischief and, once again, put himself in greater danger than he had first realised.

"Wow, this bog is wetter than I thought. Mother is going to kill me when she sees the state of my boots... I'll have to wash them in the servants' entryway and claim the dogs dragged them out in the snow..." Edward spoke to no one in particular as he trudged over the narrow patches of dry ground before him. The winter's cold nipped at him fiercely, his feet particularly feeling the effects after having been submerged up to the knees thrice already since he had started his journey. Mumbling incoherently to himself helped steel his courage, helped him to ignore the trials of the wetlands and keep himself centered on the task before him.

It was only now, deep into the boggy mire and thoroughly lost, that Edward even realised he had no idea where to search for a hibernating frog or toad. Should he be digging in the mud with his hands, or looking for mounds of leaf litter? Only brought out into the country for holidays, Edward knew little of the wildlife outside his home. He could no more recite the hibernation habits of a toad than he could tell a toad from a frog. Still, his brother had worked his way under his skin again, and Edward was determined not to return home until he had found a toad and presented it to Martin.

The further Edward ventured, the narrower and sparser the sections of dry, solid earth became. It felt like he was hop-stepping between little islands that poked out of the waters, and the frozen mud he had encountered on the edges of the wetlands had now turned wet and sludgy in these deeper recesses.

Mis-stepping twice more, Edward grumbled to himself as he hauled his left foot out of the boggy ground. The suction around his leg was incredible and he had to put real effort into pulling his leg free of the mire. He feared his boot being lost altogether and having to hop home on only one leg. However, when his leg became trapped a second time, his fears took on a more ominous turn.

As Edward's left leg sank up to his knee once more in the boggy swamp, he felt an even greater resistance as he tried to right himself. This time, he feared he was truly stuck in the mud and stranded all alone out on the fens. Panicked and yet still determined not to be defeated by the mire, Edward began to throw his whole weight this way and that, twisting his torso and reaching out to grab the roots of a nearby tree to use as an anchor as he attempted to free himself from the mud's wet clutches. He succeeded.

Throwing his weight all on one side and pulling on the tree root with all his might, Edward Stanford succeeded in hauling his leg out of the mire. However, the surprise of being free, and the lack of resistance against him, caused him to overbalance yet again. Thrown by the momentum and horribly unbalanced, Edward's body spanned over the narrow stretch of dry ground on which he stood. Time seemed to slow, and Edward seemed intensely aware of everything around him as he felt his balance tip and his whole body fall out into the deeper stretch of icy water on the farther side of him. He felt only momentary resistance against his back as the ice that frosted over the waters shattered around him. Then, all the boy knew was cold.

Eliza had her skirts hiked up, mud and dirty water dirtying her stockings and boots as she plunged through the mists to get to the shadow that had fallen into the water. Ordinarily, she could navigate the bogs without getting a single stain on her, but when every second might be the difference between rescue and death, she had no time to check her footing. She had enough intuition and presence of mind to avoid the worst of the pitfalls, ensuring she did not become trapped in the mud as the stranger had done several times before finally falling into the waters.

As she neared the spot where the poor unfortunate soul had fallen Eliza was relieved to see she was well in time to perform a rescue. Though there was no sign of the man above the waterline, the water all about was frothing and swirling wildly as the stranger thrashed amongst the reeds and mud. Eliza breathed an urgent prayer for strength, and dropped down to her knees, hands reaching into the dark, murky waters and groping blindly until she felt something hard brush against her fingers. She seized it, relief filling her when she realised she had caught the stranger by the wrists. His fingers wrapped around hers and she began to pull, careful to keep her grip on the solid earth lest she be dragged down by the panicked, drowning man.

To Eliza's welcome surprise, the victim of the mires was not at all heavy and she was able to pull the figure out onto the banks with relative ease. It was only when he was halfway out of the water, coughing and spluttering for breath that she realised it was a boy near her own age. Realising this, Eliza worked all the harder to help the lad onto the shore, sacrificing her footing a little now she knew the boy's weight wouldn't threaten to drag her down into the water with him.

As the boy opened his eyes and took in much-needed lungsful of air, he seemed to become better aware of his surroundings, working with Eliza as he engaged his hands and knees and crawled onto the shore. At last, he was on dry land. He rolled onto his back, staring up into the sky and panting profusely as his mind processed the near-death experience.

"Are you all right? What happened to you? What are you doing out here on your own? Do you have a name?"

Eliza was a whirlwind of questions as she leaned over the boy, eyes wide with fright as she looked him over for injury...

Who is this unfortunate victim of the mire? And what will come of this chance meeting? **Continue reading and delight yourself in this beautiful hope-filled Christmas tale...**

Continue Reading The Desperate Christmas Angel on Amazon

LOVE VICTORIAN CHRISTMAS SAGA ROMANCE?

If you enjoyed this story why not continue straight away with other books in our PureRead Victorian Christmas Romance library?

Read them all...

Churchyard Orphan

Orphan Christmas Miracle

Workhouse Girl's Christmas Dream

The Winter Widow's Daughter

The Match Girl & The Lost Boy's Christmas Hope

The Christmas Convent Child

The Orphan Girl's Winter Secret

Rag And Bone Winter Hope

Isadora's Christmas Plight

PLUS THESE BRAND NEW CHRISTMAS TALES
FROM OUR BESTSELLING VICTORIAN
ROMANCE AUTHORS

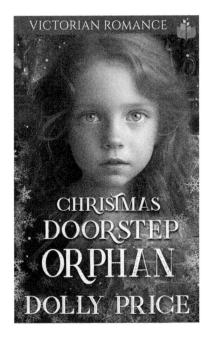

Read Christmas Doorstep Orphan on Amazon

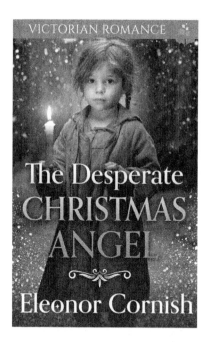

Read The Desperate Christmas Angel

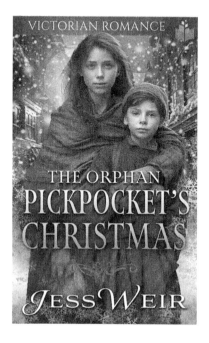

Read The Orphan Pickpocket's Christmas

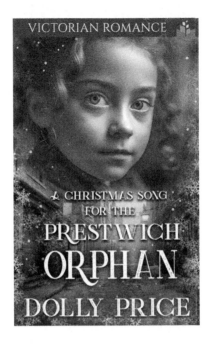

A Christmas Song For The Prestwich Orphan

OUR GIFT TO YOU

AS A WAY TO SAY THANK YOU WE WOULD LOVE TO SEND YOU THIS BEAUTIFUL STORY FREE OF CHARGE.

Our Reader List is 100% FREE

Click here for your free copy of Whitechapel Waif

PureRead.com/victorian

At PureRead we publish books you can trust. Great tales without smut or swearing, but with all of the mystery and romance you expect from a great story.

Be the first to know when we release new books, take part in our fun competitions, and get surprise free books in your inbox by signing up to our Reader list.

As a thank you you'll receive an exclusive copy of Whitechapel Waif - a beautiful book available only to our subscribers...

Click here for your free copy of Whitechapel Waif

PureRead.com/victorian

Printed in Great Britain
by Amazon

33627097R00169